Jazz House

by

D. V. Stone

Impact, Book Two

Jazz House

Cover Art by *Tina Lynn Stout*

The Wild Rose Press, Inc.
PO Box 708
Adams Basin, NY 14410-0708
Visit us at www.thewildrosepress.com

Publishing History
First Edition, 2022
Trade Paperback ISBN 978-1-5092-4338-9
Digital ISBN 978-1-5092-4339-6

Impact, Book Two
Published in the United States of America

Dedication

This book is dedicated to First Responders in all forms. The people who give up their time and often their well-being to protect and serve.

And especially to Lieutenant M. Monaco of the Newton NJ Police Department. Thank you for all the time you spent with me on the phone. I appreciate your insight which helped me with my character Michael. You and your fellow police officers have a difficult job that is often underappreciated. I hope I did justice to you all with my character Officer Michael Machau of the fictional Slate Quarry Police Department.

To my friend Getty. Each day when leaving work, everyone would get a Getty hug and be admonished to "make good choices." You are an inspiration.

To ELF—my editor, breathing coach, and cheerleader.

To my BETA readers, Paula L., Noemi D., and Amber Daulton, I couldn't have done this without you.

To Pete, my dearly beloved and biggest supporter, TWF.

And finally, to my Lord and Savior, whose blessings are new every morning.

Jordan scrambled to the other side of the limo.

"You sing good tonight." He scrolled through his phone.

"Yes, Kyrios."

Outside the window, massive cruise ships docked in the port. Happy older people made their way up the gangplanks toting bags filled with souvenirs, while the younger ones debarked dressed for the nightlife. Sparkly sequins flashed like diamonds as one young woman twirled on the pier.

God, how had she come to this life? She willed her hovering tears not to fall. Kyrios wouldn't approve.

When she was offered a place in the touring group ten years ago, she thought it was the beginning of great things. Standing in the cabaret with the lights shining down was her dream come true. When she was the woman in the sparkly dress.

Until he showed up.

Each night, Kyrios Vasilakis, Greek business tycoon, sat at the front table watching her. Yes, he was older but so very handsome. Dark hair with silver at the temples, he cut a dashing figure in his black suits.

Jordan began to sing to him. It was the beginning of the end. After a whirlwind romance, she found herself a prisoner in marriage to a brute.

Praise for D. V. Stone

Rock House Grill- Winner N. N. Light Book Award
Winner Sweet Romance.
Rock House Grill - Finalist Oklahoma Writers Guild
Rock House Grill - Author Shout Out Recommended
Read Award

Chapter 1

One year earlier

"Jordan, where are you?" Kyrios bellowed with his deep-voiced broken accent.

"I'm coming." Jordan Vasilakis swallowed and struggled to control the hated warble of nerves in her voice. She took measure of her reflection in the gilded mirror, almost not recognizing the girl she once was. Haunted gold-flecked brown eyes surrounded by black and blue stared back. She dabbed the medium-brown concealer to the fading bruise, blending it to cover her husband's response to her last perceived indiscretion.

After dropping the tube into her makeup holder, she snapped the silver bag shut. One more check. Ugh, those few stray hairs would offend him. She patted her short black bob to make sure every strand was in place and then ran down the stairs of the Mediterranean villa.

"It's about time. You know I hate being late." Kyrios waited at the bottom of the white staircase, adjusting his cuffs. "Let's go."

When he grabbed her upper arm, she flinched but didn't fight as he led her out of the air conditioning into the heat of the night and to the waiting car. "I'm sorry, Kyrios, I thought you told me eight o'clock."

A growl was his only response.

He *had* told her eight, but he liked keeping her off-balance by leaving earlier.

The driver opened the back door to the black limousine, and her husband shoved her in.

Jordan scrambled to the other side before he climbed in and could push her over.

"You sing good tonight." He scrolled through his phone. "Make me proud."

"Yes, Kyrios."

On the other side of the window, massive cruise ships docked in the port.

Happy older people made their way up the gangplanks, toting bags filled with souvenirs, while the younger ones disembarked dressed for the nightlife.

Sparkly sequins flashed like diamonds as one young woman twirled on the pier.

God, how had she come to this life? She willed her hovering tears not to fall. Kyrios wouldn't approve.

When she was offered a place in the touring group ten years ago, she thought it was the beginning of great things. Standing in the cabaret with the lights shining down was her dream come true. When *she* was the woman in the sparkly dress.

Until he showed up.

Each night, Kyrios Vasilakis, Greek business tycoon, sat at the front table watching her. Yes, he was older but so very handsome. Dark-haired with silver at the temples, he cut a dashing figure in his black suits.

Jordan began to sing to him. It was the beginning of the end. After a whirlwind romance, she found herself a prisoner in marriage to a brute.

"Why are you so difficult to please? I told you I would make you a star."

"Yes, Kyrios." No longer did she find his accent

and voice sexy. Jordan's throat tightened when his gaze focused on her. "Thank you."

"Have I not kept my promise?"

"Yes, you always keep your word." Not all of them. He promised to love and cherish her too.

"Bah, you're an ungrateful woman." He turned back to his phone. The blue-light filter made his cheekbones stand out and shadowed his face.

Jordan shrank farther into the corner. She was no star. The only places she sang were in one of Kyrios's clubs or at a business associate's party.

Since they'd married, he closed her off to everyone outside of his circle, including her family.

But it was better not to say anything. The last time she argued, he almost put her in the hospital.

When the doctor on his payroll pleaded for her to be admitted, her husband refused. He ordered the man to attend her at home.

The doctor complied.

Everyone complied.

Several minutes later, the limo pulled up to the curb outside Lunae Lucem, Kyrios's flagship nightclub.

Lines of people snaked around the corner, waiting to get in.

Blue sky-beams twisted a path into the night sky. Lit up in neon blue and purple, the club stood out like a beacon in the night. Bass pounding from inside bled into the street where those in line swayed to the beat.

The driver jogged around the car and opened the door for Kyrios. After her husband climbed out, the driver extended a white-gloved hand to assist Jordan.

Tito, her husband's bodyguard, stepped out of the crowd and whispered into Kyrios's ear as she moved back.

The hulking employee terrified her. She was glad she couldn't see his eyes through the dark glasses.

People in line gawked as Tito led them up the carpeted walkway.

A huge bouncer in black leather pants and a matching dress shirt met them. This man wore dark glasses too. The diamond in his ear flashed when it caught the light.

Kyrios grabbed her arm when the bouncer unhooked the cobalt velvet rope. "Hurry up. We need to get inside."

Jordan glanced back and saw more bodyguards close in behind them. "Is something wrong?"

Usually, Kyrios preened before the crowds. He trusted his guards to keep them safe from enemies. This time, he gave a vicious tug, causing her to stumble.

"Kyrios, please."

"Do not question me," he growled. "I said to hurry."

Cool air rushed out when the man with the earring opened the door and then stood to the side, allowing their contingent to pass through.

Bodyguards crowded them in the elevator.

Jordan backed into the corner out of the way while they spoke in hushed Greek tones. With her rudimentary knowledge of the language, she couldn't keep up with them.

The door slid open, and a maître d' met them. "This way, *Kyrie*."

At least she knew the word for sir.

The man led the way to the table always reserved in the middle of the room.

Patrons and waiters alike parted as if they were the Red Sea and her husband, Moses.

But Kyrios was no holy man.

Grigory Sokolov was already seated with his wife, Lenka.

Jordan had no idea which business the Russian pair shared with her husband.

At their approach, Grigory didn't stand but instead leaned back in his chair. "You're late. We started without you."

"I am never late." Kyrios pulled out his chair and sat. "You are never careful and always too early."

Grigory narrowed his eyes at Kyrios's cryptic statement, then turned his attention to Jordan. "Beautiful Jordan, good evening."

If Jordan's nerves weren't so on edge, she would have found his Dracula-esque greeting funny. Before she could answer, Lenka distracted her.

"Darling, you are ravishing as ever."

Lenka's kind words were at odds with the stone-cold look in her eyes. Dark-gray irises surrounded her dilated pupils, giving the impression of a shark.

Jordan sat in the plush seat, and the maître d' placed a cobalt-blue napkin on her lap. "As are you, Lenka."

"The usual, sir?" The waiter, who'd evidently drawn the short straw as their server tonight, stood at attention next to her.

Kyrios was a creature of habit. From ouzo and coke to halva and Greek coffee, he always ordered the same things. Stuffed grape leaves, chickpea soup, and moussaka rounded out the meal.

Jordan had learned to be quiet when he ordered for

both of them. She'd begun to accept this quirk shortly after they married when she asked for something else and was reprimanded. Mostly, she pushed the food around, especially on nights she was to sing.

"Yes," he responded, not even looking up at the man. "And make sure it's right."

Once finished with the pretense of friendliness, the three shut her out by speaking Russian. Whatever they discussed did not please her husband.

Several times Kyrios raised his voice, causing the other diners to sneak peeks at them.

Jordan took advantage of his distraction to enjoy her surroundings, even though going home with an angry Kyrios wasn't something to look forward to.

The elegance of the dining room contrasted sharply with the rest of the club. Crystal chandeliers lit the navy cushions with their silver embellishments, giving them high-end sophistication.

Patrons chatted in soft tones while the floor beneath her shoes picked up the beat from the EDM pounding the ceiling of the level below. Electronic dance music wasn't her favorite, but at one time, she could shake it with the best. She'd rather be down there than up here.

The waiter laid the first course on the table—grape leaves, shortly followed by soup.

Jordan lifted her spoon, then paused. The hair on her neck prickled as a man in the upper tier stared at Kyrios with blatant malice.

Noticing her attention, he turned and disappeared behind the wall.

Dinner progressed, but she had a bad feeling.

"Now, my beautiful songbird will entertain us."

Kyrios's bass voice jolted her attention back to him. She'd barely touched her food. Good thing. Singing on a full stomach wasn't conducive to a great performance. And if she didn't perform to Kyrios's expectations, he would make her pay. She flashed a stage smile. "Of course, it will be my pleasure."

Her husband nodded to the bandleader, who, in turn, signaled the orchestra.

The music quieted while the bandleader introduced her. "Ladies and gentlemen. Please welcome to the stage Lunae Lucem's premier chanteuse, Jordan Vasilakis."

Rising to her feet, Jordan placed her napkin on the chair seat.

The drummer tapped her signature intro song's tempo, and the crowd started to clap in time.

Maintaining her gracious smile, she walked toward the stage, grasping hands and greeting people. The silver-sequined dress she wore picked up the light and colors of the room. She felt like a disco ball. Peeking up once more at the upper tier, she didn't see the man who'd given her the chills and breathed a sigh of relief.

Once on stage, she lost herself channeling the woman of jazz. Her singing range was wide. From smoky, almost bass tones to high-range scat, Jordan could sing it all.

The audience loved it.

As she finished the first set, to a standing ovation, she leaned forward to take a bow.

People started screaming.

Shading her eyes from the stage lights, she scanned the room for the source.

Shots rang out. From all the exits, men in black

military-style suits rushed into the room.

Jordan scrambled and ran backstage. A burning sensation across her forehead caused her to stumble. She reached up and touched the area near her temple. It was wet. She stared in horror at the blood covering her fingers. Loud buzzing in her ears dimmed the sounds of gunshots and screaming.

"No," she murmured. "This is your chance. Take a deep breath."

The table behind the stage curtains held the remnants of someone's meal.

She grabbed a cloth napkin from it and pressed it to her face. Trying to focus, she searched for a way out. There. A door to the kitchen. She peeked through the glass in the door. All the workers had fled.

Jordan slipped into the room and darted behind the stainless-steel island. The back door was open. As she ran through it, there was a loud explosion from the direction of the dining room. The force of it pushed her out, slamming the door behind her. All thought escaped her as she lay sprawled on the ground with the wind knocked out of her. Her senses slowly seeped back. *Run, you fool!*

She scrambled to her feet and ran as if the devil were after her—pausing only long enough to glance over her shoulder.

Lunae Lucem, engulfed in an inferno, blazed and lit up the night sky.

If Kyrios lived and learned she still lived, he would be her personal demon.

But even in fear, there was hope.

Chapter 2

A small woman with short, spiked hair led Jordan through the restaurant toward the back hallway. They passed through the luxurious red-and-gold appointed room.

Jordan glanced at the stage where, if she were lucky, she'd be performing soon.

"Here you are. Olivia and Shay are expecting you."

"Thank you." Whoops, Jordan's tummy rumbled at the smells coming from the kitchen. She skipped breakfast that morning. Her nerves couldn't handle the thought of food.

"Good luck," the woman called over her shoulder as she headed back the way they'd come.

"Thanks." Standing outside the door, Jordan rubbed her hands together, trying to warm them. Her nerves, coupled with Northeast Pennsylvania's cold, chilled deep into her marrow.

After escaping Kyrios, she'd worked her way across Europe as a waitress. When she earned enough cash for a fake ID and plane ticket to the States, she didn't know where to go. Not home. Putting her family in danger wasn't an option. Now here she was, in Slate Quarry, Pennsylvania, living in a cheap apartment, jobless and friendless.

Buck up, girlfriend. It's time to take back your life. Or some form of it. She rapped on the door to Jazz

House's office.

"Just a minute."

A beat later, the knob turned, and the door cracked open.

Hazel-colored eyes peered out from under a baseball-capped head. "Hi, you must be Madeline Cielo. I'm Shay McDowell, Jazz House's chef. Come in."

"Yes, I'm Madeline." Jordan hoped she sounded normal. She was still getting used to her new identity.

Walking into the room, she made eye contact with the other woman, whom she recognized from pictures on the Internet—Olivia House-Errapel, owner of Jazz House. The person she needed to impress to get the job. "Ms. House."

"It's Olivia." The slim blonde woman rose from her desk and came around, extending her hand. "I'm excited to meet you. Please sit. We're both captivated by the recording of your singing."

"Thank you." Jordan perched on the edge of a red chair. "I'm glad you enjoyed it. It's a sampling of my various jazz styles."

"You have quite a range." The chef, Shay, leaned on the corner of Olivia's desk.

The two women appeared comfortable with each other.

"Anyone want coffee?"

"I'd love a cup." It would help warm Jordan and give her something to do with her hands.

Olivia nodded. "Me too."

"My kind of group." Shay went to a sideboard where the fixings were already set up.

A few minutes later, Jordan clutched a steaming

mug of cinnamon coffee. "Thank you. This is exactly what I needed. I didn't remember how cold it could get up here in the northeast."

"Are you familiar with Northeast Pennsylvania?" Shay sat in the chair next to Jordan. "Where are you from?"

"I'm from all over." Jordan sipped the coffee. "I've passed through the northeast, but it's been a while."

"Tell us about yourself, Madeline." Olivia chimed in. "Your resume shows some experience. Can you give us more details and how you see bringing this experience to Jazz House?"

Jordan's stomach churned at the thought of lying to these women. But there was nothing else she could do. She only hoped the money spent on a new identity was worth the cost. Painting on a smile, she channeled her inner Jazz Woman. "Well, let's see. I grew up in the church singing."

She'd practiced her story and built an imaginary life as the only child of estranged parents from San Bernardino. One with no roots due to parents who moved often.

"After I sang in bars and clubs, a cruise line offered me a job on a ship." With a shaky hand, she set her cup on the side table. "Life at sea wasn't something I enjoyed. When a passenger offered me a job in a Hong Kong supper club, I took it. Now, here I am." She wound up the story.

An hour later, Jordan still struggled to think of herself as Madeline. She couldn't slip up. From now on, she needed to become Madeline Cielo. Jordan Vasilakis was dead. That person had to be left in the past. Madeline was her future.

"Wow." Shay looked at her agog. "Talk about an exciting life."

"Sometimes…" Jordan choked up. "Sometimes, though, you need to come home."

"And your family?"

"I don't see them anymore." Bile rose in the back of her throat. "It's too difficult. For personal reasons, I needed to cut them out of my life."

Silence reigned for a few minutes.

Since meeting them, Jordan was sure of one thing. She liked these two.

"I was alone for a long time too." Shay's eyes took on a sheen like she was going to cry.

And if she did, Jordan wouldn't be able to hold back her own sobs. She straightened her spine. "It's for the best."

Instead of crying, Shay rose from her chair and walked around the desk and, with her arms now wrapped around Olivia, said, "Then I met this woman. She and her brother welcomed me into the family."

"And we're one big happy family." Olivia reached up and patted the other woman's cheek. "Shay and my brother Aden just got engaged, so it will soon be official. Show her the rock, Sis."

Blushing, Shay held out her hand.

Jordan gasped. "That is so beautiful. And unusual. What kind of stone is that?"

"It's a green sapphire set in rose gold." Her cheeks grew even redder. "Aden says it reminded him of my eyes."

Oh, how Jordan wanted a love that would make her cheeks heat up like that. "That is so romantic."

"Now, back to business. Madeline, we'd be lucky

to have you." Olivia sipped her coffee. "If you're interested in joining us, you'll find yourself part of the House family. We can be a little hard to take at times, but we love each other. Fiercely."

"I second it." Shay beamed at Olivia and then at Jordan. "What do you say? Are you ready to sign on to your next adventure?"

"Do you have a contract?"

Olivia opened the drawer in her desk, pulled out a blue folder, and slid it across the mahogany surface. "It's a pretty standard *Music Performance Agreement*."

She flipped through it. It looked straightforward. "The salary is generous. Meals included. Nice."

"Yes, and they won't disappoint." Olivia interrupted. "Shay is one of the finest chefs I know."

Jordan's tummy grumbled. "I can't wait. The smell of that Creole holy trinity has had my mouth watering since I walked in. Onions, celery, and carrots are a tough-to-beat combination."

She continued to peruse the contract. *Uh-oh.* Publicity and photos. That could be a deal-breaker. "There's one sticking point for me."

Olivia picked up her tortoiseshell cheater-glasses. "What's that? I'm sure we can negotiate any problems."

"I have a phobia of having my picture taken." *It's not really a lie.* "Irrational, I know, but very real. Besides, I wouldn't want my—" She swallowed hard. "—family to know where I am."

"What about smoky silhouettes." Shay pulled off her cap and tapped it on her knee. "I've seen pictures done like that. Very sexy. Very mysterious. Only shadows and smoke."

Jordan winked and pointed at Shay. "I can work

with that idea. Where do I sign?"

A moment of panic nearly closed her throat when she almost signed the contract with her correct name. Luckily, her M and J both began with a curl.

"Where are you staying?" Olivia gathered up the papers. "Do you have a place yet?"

"Right now, I have a room at Hilde's Luchtbed."

"I remember when we called them boarding houses. Everyone is so fancy now." Shay walked to the door. "You two can finish up any details. My kitchen is calling me. It was nice meeting you, Madeline."

"Nice to meet you too." After Shay left, Jordan turned back to her new boss. "Okay, when do I start?"

"As soon as possible." Olivia got up and began to pace the room. "I'll set up a photo session. We'll get some old-fashioned headliner posters made up. I want to keep the look of the old jazz clubs. Will you help me find the band?"

"Sure. I play several instruments." Jordan tapped her fingers on the arm of the chair. "We need to take our time finding the right people. Until we interview, if you like, I could begin alone playing the piano and singing."

"Can you help me find the musicians to interview?"

"We could hit clubs and listen. May I have paper and a pen?"

Olivia handed them over, and she began a list. "Online is also a good way to go. Social media sites host lots of people recording and making videos."

Jordan handed a comprehensive to-do list back to her boss. "It looks like a lot, but I can help. Lists and organization are my thing. A bit compulsive, but I like order."

"Me too." Olivia placed the pad and pen on the desk. "How about a tour of Jazz House. Are you hungry?"

"If I can have some of whatever that smell is." Jordan closed her eyes and inhaled. "I'd love to tour the Jazz House. What I've seen so far is stunning. Exactly the way someone would imagine an early-1900's club."

Once in the hallway, Olivia opened a door across from her office. "This is the band room. There's a private bathroom so you can get ready here or touch up between sets and have some privacy."

Jordan was surprised when she stepped into the comfortably appointed room. The design from the outer space carried through. "Wow, usually the performers get a converted closet or nothing."

"My brother, Aden, and I take care of our employees." Olivia opened the door to the roomy bathroom. "We believe that if we treat everyone well, they'll be happy to work here and give us their best."

"There's another restaurant, right?" Jordan checked out the more-than-adequate lighting on the mirrored dressing table. A clothing rack stood against one wall, and she could imagine her dresses hanging from it. The place even had a shower. "Your brother runs that one?"

"Yes. Rock House is a different style, as you can tell by the name, but the philosophy is the same. Great food, wonderful service, and music. Really good music." Her new boss went on. "Our pastry chef, Margaret, and her chef husband Eli are our business partners. They're part of our family as well."

Olivia paused.

Jordan turned to see why she'd stopped talking and

was caught up in Olivia's brown-eyed gaze.

"Our staff tends to become family. A family who will stand by you and support you." She shrugged. "Sometimes, blood's not thicker than water."

Jordan forced down the burning in the back of her throat. As much as she'd like to be someone's family again, she couldn't risk it. "Thanks. Please don't be offended, but I keep to myself. I'm a loner and comfortable with it."

"We'll see." Dark-brown eyes, similar to Jordan's own, held her gaze for a long moment. It seemed like Olivia peered into Jordan's soul.

The awkward moment passed, and Olivia rose. "Come on, let's check out the stage and then steal some food from under Shay's nose."

The stage took up the inside corner of Jazz House. There was a small platform big enough for her and maybe a trio. Jordan ran her hand over the gleaming baby grand piano. "It's digital?"

"Yes, I was assured it feels and plays like the acoustic."

"May I?" Excitement she hadn't experienced in a long time bubbled in her. "I've never played a digital this nice."

"Absolutely. I'll be over there." Olivia walked to the bar and sat.

Turning her full attention to the piano, Jordan examined the digital panel, which ran the keyboard's length. She located the switch. Her fingers, as if with a mind of their own, confidently flowed over the keys. It was surprising how much like the acoustic version it felt.

Once she became accustomed to the key action, her

muse took over, and a bluesy ballad of lost youth and love took form. By the second verse, she found herself singing along—the sad words nearly choking her.

As the song's notes died off, Jordan paused to get herself under control. Tears were a private thing. She refused to let them escape. When she did look over toward the bar, Olivia was no longer alone.

****

The investigator blanched and peered past Kyrios's shoulder. "Yes, *Kyrie*. All the bodies are accounted for. Your woman is not among them."

"Get out." Spittle gathered in the corner of Kyrios's mouth. "Find my wife."

"Yes, Kyrie." The man scuttled toward the door.

Kyrios picked up the paperweight Jordan had given to him shortly after their wedding day. It held a picture of the two of them. He hurled it across the room.

It shattered.

Tito stepped out of the corner. A fresh livid scar ran down his face from temple to chin. "Your orders?"

"Make sure she is found," he snarled. "Do whatever is necessary to reacquire my wife."

Tito nodded and left the room.

He glared, looking around for something else to break. How dare she? He stomped to his desk, grabbed his cell phone, and dialed.

"Hello, sir. How may I be of assistance?" His lawyer answered on the first ring.

"Have my marriage to Jordan annulled." Kyrios offered no greeting. "Effective the day of the explosion."

The man stuttered on the other end. He said, "Annul? A dead woman?"

"She's not dead," he bellowed. "At least not yet." Then he threw the phone against the wall too. Standing with feet apart and hands clenched, he panted, staring at the pieces until the phone on his burnished ebony-wood desk trilled.

He stalked over and smoothed his white slacks before settling into one of the matching oversized black leather chairs. The phone continued to ring, but he let his secretary wait. The man knew he was in there. On the eleventh ring, he hit the button. "What?"

"Kyrie"—the balding man's voice shook—"I have Grigory Sokolov on the line."

Kyrios clenched his teeth, stared up at the ceiling, and exhaled. Sokolov grew intolerable. "Wait two minutes before putting him through. No, three. And get me a new mobile phone immediately."

He hit the disconnect button, shoved back in his chair, and glared at the picture frame on the desk.

Jordan's smiling face mocked him.

"*Stríngla.*" He slammed it facedown with a curse.

She wasn't like all the other women—insipid, ridiculous, and easily manipulated. Females were nothing but to please a man. When they stopped? Easily replaced. But this one? She would make a fool of him.

The light on the phone blinked. Another thing pecking at him. Grigory. How long must he suffer his father's old partner? The man stopped being important long ago. It was only to honor his *patéras* he pretended to listen to Grigory's counsel. Now it was time to take the contact information and make the law and the law's enforcers, the *astynomía,* work for him without a go-between.

"Grigory, what can I do for you, old friend?" His

tone oozed feigned amity.

"Kyrios, what are you doing approaching the Americans without me?" The older man whined then coughed. Since the fire, his cigarette-damaged lungs wheezed. "You should keep me appraised. We are business partners, are we not?"

The Americans in the state of Pennsylvania were receptive to Kyrios's proposals. The plans and trip were already in the beginning stages.

"Of course we are." His sneer wasn't apparent in his cajoling reply. "Always. It was simply an oversight. A courier will be dispatched this afternoon with all the information." He grimaced at the coughing over the phone line.

"Good." Grigory panted. "We wouldn't want animosity between us, would we?"

"Enjoy your afternoon, my old friend." Kyrios hung up and rubbed his forehead. It was time to end this charade.

There was a light knock at the door.

"Enter." He glanced at his secretary. "Do you have my phone?"

"Yes, Kyrie." The wiry man in a business suit with a stark-white shirt and thin tie hurried over. "Security assures me it exceeds all your expectations."

"It should." Kyrios grabbed the phone and started scrolling through it. "Has Tito returned?"

"Yes, Kyrie."

"Send him in."

The man scurried back to the outer office.

Seconds later, Tito loomed in the doorway.

"Come in and shut the door. I have another job for you." Kyrios pulled a cigar from the desktop humidor, cut, and lit it. "Our old friend Grigory is failing. Make sure he rests. Am I understood?"

An impassive nod.

"Lenka might take it hard. Make sure she has her— medication."

One more nod.

"Go and get it done." He poured a tsipouro and raised it in mock salute. "Rest, *old friend*."

Chapter 3

"What do you mean Kayla Lane was released?" Officer Michael Machau slammed his hand onto the desk. "It's been months, and no one stepped forward to make bail."

Lieutenant Jeff Morgan gave him a back-off look. The lieutenant's office, like his desk, was immaculate. "I know you're close to the victim's family, but you need to be professional."

Michael tucked his mirrored aviator sunglasses into his shirt collar and threw himself into the chair across from the neat desk. "For crying out loud, she shot Nick Bianchi. I don't like Bianchi, but he's a cop."

"Was a cop." Lt. Morgan twirled his pen like a majorette with a baton. "We spoke this morning. He's not returning to duty. Said he needs to get his life in order."

"So, the nutcase destroys a career. And she gets away with it."

"Lane isn't getting away with anything." Morgan pointed the pen at Michael. "We both know Nick was well on the road to self-destruction."

"The House family is still dealing with Olivia's attack." Michael ran his hands through his hair. Man, he needed a cut. "Who bailed Lane out?"

"Some guy named Atticus Jones. He's a food critic."

"How does he have a hundred thousand for bail?" Michael sputtered, and his pulse pounded in his ears. "What's his connection?"

Morgan flipped open the file. "He took out a bond, so only had to come up with ten percent. No idea what the connection is except the restaurant angle."

"I want to be kept in the loop." Michael stood and leaned in, pressing his palms to the desktop. "Who's keeping an eye on Kayla Lane?"

His superior slammed the folder closed. "You know we don't have that kind of manpower."

"Perfect, she walks around free?" He threw his hands up.

"That's what bail is, Officer Machau." The lieutenant stared back at him. "Keep your distance from the suspect."

"Fine." Michael slapped his hands on the desk and straightened. He winced at his flash of petty gladness at the handprints he'd left behind on the shiny surface. Then he turned and stalked to the door.

"Machau."

Morgan's voice stopped him in the doorway.

"Unofficially, stay close to your people. You keep me in the loop too. Understand?"

Michael looked back, nodded, slid his aviators on, and closed the door.

Some of the other cops stared at him with varying expressions of surprise.

Typically, he was a pretty even-tempered guy. His voice must have carried.

"You all right there, Machau?" Sergeant Allyssa Romano stood blocking the steel doors leading into the parking lot. "Need an ear?"

"Nah. Thanks, Sarge." He pulled the sunglasses down and peered at her over them. "I'm good."

"If you do, you know where to find me." With a curt nod, she moved out of the way and barked at a nearby rookie. "What are you staring at? Get back to work and fix your report."

Michael pushed the glasses back up and ducked out, hiding a smile. The sergeant could be like a Doberman. Loud bark and sharp teeth when you messed up, but also kind and supportive—protective of her cops. The rookie must've royally screwed up. While walking to his police car, he pulled his cell out and pressed Aden's contact. "Hey, something's come up. Can you meet me at Jazz House?"

"Why? Is everything all right?" Aden growled in Michael's ear.

The man had the right to be jumpy after last summer and fall. Between his car accident and Kayla Lane's vicious attacks on his sister, Shay, and the business, Michael often wondered how he'd stayed such a good guy.

"What's going on?" Aden pushed. "Is anyone hurt?"

"Nobody's hurt. No sense in arguing nor repeating the story. I'll tell you when you get there." Michael ended the call, stuck the phone into his pocket, and walked to the patrol car. Jazz House was only a few miles away, so he'd be there in a couple of minutes.

Coming up the highway ramp, he snorted at all the speeders hitting their brakes.

Route 84 was often like the Autobahn in Germany. Drivers went as fast as they could and tried not to get caught.

But right now, he was buried in a pack of law-abiding citizens doing barely fifty-five. He stayed with the pack until the exit. A few city-blocks later, Jazz House's brick façade and black awning came into view. Excellent, there was a spot to park right in front.

No one greeted Michael as he walked in. Soulful sounds of a piano caressed his ears, drawing him into the dining room.

Olivia sat enraptured at the bar, peering at the stage.

Madeline's sultry voice joined the notes.

He yanked off his glasses when he almost tripped over a chair on his way over to Olivia. All his attention focused on the gorgeous woman singing one of the saddest songs he ever heard. "Who's she?"

"That, my friend, is Jazz House's new singer."

"What's her name?" Michael couldn't take his eyes off her. He kept missing when he tried to hang the glasses from the neck of his shirt.

"Madeline Cielo." Olivia sighed. "She's amazing, right?"

"Amazing and beautiful." His heart banged against his chest wall. She was the most gorgeous woman he'd ever seen—from her smooth brown complexion to her luscious red lips. Short black hair framed her oval face. And her voice? Angels would sing like that.

"Officer Machau, are you smitten?" Olivia teased. "I can't blame you—hey, why are you here in uniform?"

The notes to the song drifted away, and the woman bowed her head. When she lifted it, her tawny gaze landed on Michael. A wide, panicked expression passed over her when she took in his blue uniform. Quick as it came, her expression turned bland.

"Michael, why are you here?" Olivia touched his arm.

Aden came crashing through the door, his metal cane thumping the floor as he crossed the room. "What's going on?"

"I want you both to remain calm." Michael patted Olivia's hand, then said to Aden, "Get Shay. She needs to hear this too."

Aden limped to the kitchen door. His injury from last year's car accident was still mending. He returned seconds later with Shay tucked under his arm as she wiped her hands on a towel.

"Hey, Michael. What's the ruckus about?" she asked.

"Kayla made bail."

"What do you mean, she made bail?" Aden yelled and slapped the bar top. "After all the trouble she caused? My sister is still recovering from that witch hitting her in the head. Kayla pointed a gun at the woman I love." He kissed the top of Shay's head. "She needs to be locked up forever."

"No, no, no. That can't be right." Olivia swayed then plopped onto the barstool. "They can't have let Kayla out.

"I don't know why." Michael put his hand on Aden's shoulder, but the man shrugged it off.

"Aden." Shay chided him gently while slipping out from her fiancé's embrace and hurrying over to Olivia. "It's not Michael's fault."

"How?" Olivia slumped farther and touched the side of her temple, where Kayla had slammed her with a heavy kitchen pot. "How can she be out of jail after all she's done?"

Shay slipped a hand around Olivia's arm. "Michael, help me get her into the office. Aden, call David."

"No." Olivia straightened and stood. "I'm fine, Shay. Let me go. Don't bother David at the hospital. He's busy."

Aden glanced up from his cell. "Are you sure? Your husband would want to know what's going on."

"*I* don't even know what's going on."

Michael glanced back to the gorgeous woman across the room he'd spotted when he came in.

She stood staring at them wide-eyed.

"Let's take this into the office," he said.

Olivia nodded, glancing at the newcomer. "Madeline, I'm sorry. Can you come back tomorrow? I'll explain everything."

"Sure."

The woman looked ready to bolt anyway.

She gathered her coat and hat from the rack in the corner. "See you tomorrow. I hope everything's okay."

Michael couldn't help staring at her retreating figure until she disappeared through the vestibule.

"Let's go. Everyone in the office." Aden hobbled toward the door.

After they all filed in, Olivia, pale and shaking, took a seat at the desk. "Okay, catch us up."

Shay hovered over her while Aden leaned on his cane and began to pace the carpet with an uneven gait.

Michael stood out of the way near the door. When Aden paced, you didn't want to get run over. "There's not much to catch up." He fiddled with his hat. "My supervisor called me into his office a little while ago.

He knows we're friends. Said Kayla was out."

Aden banged the cane on the floor. "I want to know who? Who bailed her out?"

"Since it's a matter of public record, I can tell you." Michael glanced at Olivia. "The guy's name is Atticus Jones."

"The food critic?" She flinched as if struck and began blinking rapidly.

"You know him?"

"He hates me. Hates Jazz House." Olivia opened her computer. "*The Restaurant Auditor* is one of the most popular blog sites in Slate Mill and the surrounding areas. Atticus Jones, the author, hates us."

Michael dodged Aden and went around the desk.

A man sporting blond pompadoured hair and black-framed glasses was plastered on the blog site's banner. The guy looked like a snake with his pretentious façade and smarmy smile. "Why does he hate you?"

"We don't know." She slammed the lid on the laptop. "He's alone. Most of the other critics love my restaurant."

"Jazz House isn't a failure," Shay interrupted. "One man can't dictate our success. Across the board, other critics praise the restaurant and say it's the place to be."

"When was the man even here?" Aden finally stopped pacing and sat down. "What's his connection to Kayla."

"Obviously, the connection is enough for him to fork over a lot of money." A tic began in Michael's jaw. He had many acquaintances but few close buddies. He'd lived as a loner on the fringes, but the people in this room had become his friends. The past months they'd embraced him like a brother. No one was going to hurt them if he had anything to do with it. "You all need to keep your eyes open. No one goes out alone. You know the drill from last time."

"I hate this." Olivia leaned back in her chair. "Kayla Lane needs to go back to jail so we can lead our lives."

"Now, let's run this down." Michael took out his notepad. "Jones is connected to the restaurant world, but is there something deeper?"

****

Mindful of the patchy spots of ice, Jordan navigated the short distance home to her rented room. She'd evaluated all the job opportunities and decided northeastern Pennsylvania seemed the safest. Why would anyone look for her there? The bigger cities? Maybe. Here? Unlikely. Always cautious, she'd gotten into town two weeks before the interview to check things out, observing the neighborhood and both Jazz and Rock House.

Glancing left and right, she dashed across the street, dancing out of the way of the splash of slush from the city bus.

She stuck her key into the lock of the apartment house's main door.

The old Victorian building had once been a doctor's home and practice. Now it was comprised of small studios on each of the two upper floors.

Wiping her feet on the mat, she checked the mailbox in the vestibule and then entered the hallway. Low tones of a TV came from 1A.

Laura, the owner, lived on the first floor and took

good care of the place. The woman loved competition shows. It didn't matter whether they were cooking, dancing, or singing. Tonight, it was singing, and whoever was performing did a great job with the cover song.

Jordan began to hum along. Maybe she could incorporate that music into her act. She trailed her hand along the polished mahogany banister as she trotted up the stairs.

The second floor had two apartments. One neighbor kept to herself, only nodding when they passed in the hall. The other, a guy, was a bit too friendly.

She stopped humming and tiptoed past his door, hoping he wasn't home. She had a feeling he watched through the peephole. Creep.

On the third floor, the fancy woodwork gave way to a more-utilitarian style. This was where the house workers used to live.

Nothing fancy, but even though it was plain, it suited her needs and was the only apartment on this floor.

A quick run of her hand around the doorframe assured her the invisible tape remained intact. Once inside, she closed the door, locked it, and slid the chain into place. Her keys clattered into the bowl on the table.

This one-room apartment was the closest thing she had to a safe place. Before she signed the lease, she asked Laura about upgrading the security. As long as it didn't cost the landlady anything, the woman was okay with it.

Jordan bought the best she could afford, which wasn't much. A window alarm by the fire escape, and a camera looking into the hallway alerted her phone. And last, a deadbolt and old-fashioned chain for the door. Funny how the chain gave her comfort.

She needed assurance. Her nerves were still rattled from seeing the police officer with Olivia. The newspaper articles she read about the Houses didn't say anything about trouble with the law, only about the brother's accident.

Could she have missed something?

A shiver ran down her spine. A hot cup of tea would calm her as well as chase away the chill. She filled the kettle from the small sink next to the college-size refrigerator included with the apartment.

Rounding out the kitchen was a microwave sitting on a baker's rack alongside a toaster and small bistro set.

While the electric kettle began to do its thing, she grabbed her mug and the box of herbal tea from the cabinet above the sink.

In the three minutes it took for the kettle to boil, she grabbed her pj's and robe. Faster than a superhero in a phone booth, she changed into warm pajamas and woolly socks.

The kettle howled for attention.

Chamomile tea in hand, she sat on the small sofa and scrolled through her phone. Opening the search engine, instead of typing in Jazz House this time, she tried Olivia House. On the second page of responses, she found the article from a few months ago.

Olivia House, part owner and manager of Rock House Grill, needed medical attention after an attack at the soon-to-open Jazz House. Representatives say Ms.

House is stable and expected to make a complete recovery.

A few clicks later, Jordan found the rest of the story.

Kayla Lane, a former hostess at Rock House Grill, was arrested yesterday. She is charged with violations ranging from criminal trespass to assault with a deadly weapon. Other charges are expected to follow after a full investigation. Crimes of assault and battery, arson, as well as giving false reports to police, and vandalism may be added. Police are looking for conspirators.

Lane is housed at the Slate Quarry County Jail. Bail set at one-hundred-thousand dollars. She has requested a public defender.

Jordan leaned back and set her cup down. Eyes closed, she rubbed her forehead. Stay? Go? She signed the contract, but it was under Madeline Cielo. Olivia agreed to no pictures.

"I like them." The sound of her voice was loud in the empty room. Could she stay and put down roots? Or was it only a pipe dream? The focus wouldn't be on her. What would be the harm in remaining for a couple of weeks? If things heated up, she could always slip away. She'd become accustomed to this way of life. Besides, Kyrios was half the world away.

She pulled the crocheted granny square afghan off the back of the sofa. It reminded her of the one her mother had back home. Multi-hued patches in all the colors of the rainbow were stitched together with black yarn. It warmed and comforted her. Lying down, wrapped in the poor imitation of home, she flipped channels on the TV until she fell asleep.

Chapter 4

Buzzing from her phone woke Jordan from a dreamless sleep. She blinked and looked at the screen. Ten a.m. "Hello, Olivia."

"Sorry to call so early. I hope I didn't wake you?"

"No, I was awake." *Liar*.

"I found an open-mic tonight at a Scranton music house. They're known for attracting top-notch talent."

"Wow, that was quick."

"Aden can join us. I'd appreciate his input. Would you mind?"

Hmm, with the House siblings to herself, maybe she could feel out the situation better. "Sounds good. What time do they start? Nine?"

"Yes, Aden will pick us up at eight. What's your address?"

The fewer people coming in and out of the apartment building, the better. "I'll meet you at Jazz House. I'd like to hang around a bit and get a feel for the customers, if that's all right."

"Sure. I'll see you tonight."

Jordan hung up. There was a public library a few blocks away. After her shower, she'd head there and pick up some new reading material. She could use their computers to research some more talent. Phones were great, but nothing beat research on a bigger screen.

An hour later, Madeline Cielo was a card-carrying

member of the Slate Quarry Public Library. After signing up at the desk to use one of the computers, she browsed the racks looking for a good novel. Medical mysteries were her favorite, and if there was some romance, all the better.

With several possibilities in hand, she read the inside covers of the first two. When a seat became vacant at the computer bank, she gathered up her books. After she clicked to agree to terms and policies, the world was now at her fingertips. She fired up the search engine.

As painful as it was, she looked up Kyrios's name every few days. It didn't stop her intake of breath when his face cleared on the screen. Age was catching up with him. But even so, the gray at his temples looked distinguished. He'd become a little jowly this past year but was still an attractive man. For the most part, he remained in Greece. Always with a new woman on his arm. The merry widower.

Jordan clicked on the articles. Nothing new on the horizon. No red flags raised.

On to the Houses. By six p.m., she'd learned they both were respected members of not only the community but the restaurant world. There were a couple of blips around the time of Aden's accident. It seemed the ex-girlfriend was a piece of work. The other anomaly was Atticus Jones and his blog, *The Restaurant Auditor*.

When she found nothing threatening to reveal her identity, Jordan wiped the browsing history and checked out her books. The short walk to Jazz House cleared away her computer-brain and brightened her spirits.

The restaurant was already abuzz with activity, and she approached the reservation desk in the entranceway with a smile. "Olivia House is expecting me. I'm Madeline."

"Yes, she told me you were coming." The hostess dressed in a period silver flapper outfit mirrored the smile. "I'm Jess. If you need anything, let me know. Olivia is with Shay in the kitchen."

"Thanks, I will." Jordan walked through the archway into the main room and stopped to take it all in.

Smooth jazz played in the background. Waitstaff bustled about the room wearing matching black vests and pants, offset by ruby-red shirts underneath. They neither stood out nor blended in, only complemented the simple elegance of the room. The mahogany bar was the centerpiece.

If she closed her eyes, she could conjure a picture of clubs from the heyday of jazz.

Her stomach growled. The coffee and yogurt from this morning was long gone. The smells emanating from the kitchen area woke the beast. And the beast was hungry. Eyeing the stage while she made her way to the kitchen, she almost collided with a waiter carrying a tray of drinks.

He deftly balanced the tray, apologized, and moved on before she could say she was sorry.

Peeking through the porthole window into the kitchen, she made sure the coast was clear before pushing in.

It wasn't a big kitchen, but the staff moved in a tight and efficient way, somehow avoiding collisions.

Olivia stood with Shay. Both women bent over a

stainless-steel table, going over something.

"Don't worry about leaving," Shay assured Olivia. "Jess will be fine covering. It's Tuesday, so not a busy night."

"Not a busy night?" Jordan raised her eyebrows at the two women. "Looks happening to me."

"If you're hungry, grab a plate from over there, and Sophie will help you out." Olivia waved her over. "Sophie, please set Madeline up with some food?"

"Yes, Olivia." A small, tattooed pixie-like woman with pink hair and a hoop in her nose popped up beside her. "Come with me, Madeline. You don't want to get in the way of those two when they're on a roll."

Bemused, Jordan let Sophie lead her to the side counter, where she grabbed a dish. In awe, she watched the line cook create a work of art on a plate.

Sophie kept up a one-sided commentary all the while. "Shay hit the market this morning early. She scored some catfish, and this is her first try at soul food. Miss Margaret, from Rock House, worked with her on some recipes from her time living in South Carolina."

A pile of Carolina dirty rice joined fried catfish.

"Are those cracker crumbs?"

"Yes, ma'am." Sophie grinned up at her. "Tonight is old school. When Shay gets comfortable, she'll start fooling around and put her own twist in, but for tonight we get it down-home."

Honeyed cornbread and hush puppies topped the plate.

Jordan pointed to the next table. "Is that what I think it is?"

"Banana pudding if you clean your plate." Sophie eyed the pudding. "Miss Margaret makes most of the desserts for Jazz House too. At least until we find a pastry chef."

"Jazz's history is deep in the South. I fell in love while visiting Louisiana years ago." Olivia came up behind them. "Manny, my fiancé at the time, traveled with me to several southern locations, then up through St. Louis and Chicago."

"Those are great places to get your feet wet." Jordan glanced at her plate. "Looks like Shay's got a grip on the food. You seem to have one on the restaurant."

"And you're going to wrangle the music." Olivia took her elbow and guided her to the bar in the dining room. "We'll be a triple threat. Relax and enjoy your food. I have a few things to go over with the hostess before Aden arrives."

****

"You're sure you don't mind me tagging along?" Michael met Aden at the front door.

"Nah," Aden answered. "The more, the merrier."

Michael stepped into Jazz House first, then stopped in his tracks.

Aden thumped into him. "Dude, no sudden stops." He brushed past him. "I'm still not too steady on my legs."

"Sorry," Michael said absently.

"Whatever, man." Aden shook his head. "I'm going to find my sister."

"Okay."

All Michael's attention focused on the woman sitting at the bar talking to one of the servers. He walked over, taking his time enjoying the sight of her, from her curves in the black sweater to a trim waist, down to her black-jeaned bottom sitting on the stool. A chunky boot heel hooked the rail while her other leg swung free.

Jordan spotted him in the bar mirror and followed his approach with big unfathomable eyes. When he stood behind her, she turned and looked up, her expression inscrutable. "Hello."

Words stuck in his throat. He cleared it. "Hello, I'm Michael Machau, a friend of Aden's and Olivia's. We haven't officially met."

A slim rich-brown hand reached out. "I'm Madeline Cielo. I'm the new…"

"I know. Sorry, I didn't mean to interrupt, but I saw you the other day." *Shut up, Machau.* He was babbling like a teenager. "I wanted to meet you then, but things got in the way."

"Well, problem solved. Now we've met." She extracted her hand and casually picked up a napkin.

The woman was cool and put together, unlike him. He wiped his sweaty palm against his jeans. "Sorry."

"Hey, guys. Almost ready?" Aden, with Olivia beside him, kept Michael from making a further fool of himself. "Madeline, I hope you don't mind. I asked Michael to join us."

First, there was a fleeting hesitation, and then a dazzling smile wiped away any hint of concern. "Absolutely. We're becoming friends."

Heat rose from his chest up his neck, and even the tips of his ears warmed. Good thing the ambiance in Jazz House called for dark lighting. Friends—ugh. No way he wanted to be relegated to the friend zone. Michael returned her smile and took her hand. He smiled back. "Friends."

He kissed her knuckles and enjoyed the little gasp she let out.

"All right, Mr. Suave, we need to get a move on." Aden slapped him on the back.

Pulling her hand from his, Jordan blinked rapidly. She glanced at Olivia, who regarded him with raised eyebrows.

Geez, did he just come across as a creep? Michael shoved his hands in his pockets. "Right."

Lucky for him any further conversation was cut off when the hostess filling in tonight stepped up, holding Olivia and Madeline's coats.

After a few false starts where the Houses greeted a couple of regulars and introduced Madeline as the soon-to-be headliner of Jazz House, they made it outside.

Big fat snowflakes drifted down sparkling in the vintage lantern streetlights.

Madeline tilted her head back and smiled. She nearly looked angelic in a magical moment.

"Not used to snow?" he asked.

Glistening brown eyes turned to look at him. "Not really."

"Where are you from?" He thought the question innocent enough until she flinched and averted her eyes.

Olivia interceded by hooking her arm through Michael's and leading him to the other side of the van. "Women like mystery, Officer." She teased before lowering her voice for him only. "Madeline's private. She doesn't like to talk about herself."

Instead of sitting up front with Aden, Olivia sat in the back with Michael.

Before Madeline got in, he whispered in her ear.

"I'm not going to attack her, you know."

"Trust me."

When Madeline climbed into the front and buckled in, the look she gave Olivia over the seat couldn't have been more filled with relief than if she'd said the words.

His heart sank, and he stared out of the window.

Nope, not a chance with her.

The story of his life. *What's the point of even trying?* All he ever wanted was someone to love and love him back. Becca in college. Then Shay. They always wanted someone better than him. If he could be more like Aden. *Now that guy is relaxed and cool around women. Enough so, even the ever-practical Shay fell for him. Why would a gorgeous, talented, self-assured Madeline Cielo want to be with me?*

"Michael." Olivia poked him in the ribs. "We're almost there. Where are you?"

"Just thinking." *Actually wallowing.* He straightened up in the seat. Enough. He wasn't a quitter. No time like the present to grow a pair.

Worry caused an adorable little V between Olivia's perfect eyebrows. Eyebrows, how did women do that? Even Madeline's were a perfect arch.

"Hey, there's a spot opening up right out front." Aden slowed and put on the blinker. "This is going to be a lucky night."

When Michael glanced up, Aden shot him a wink. It was going to be a long night.

Aden parallel parked, and the women climbed out.

Michael handed him his cane through the split between the seats.

"Thanks, man." He glanced again at Michael in the rearview. "She's beautiful, I get it. Olivia mentioned she has some unknown baggage, so go easy."

"For crying out loud." Michael rolled his eyes heavenward. "You and your sister think I'm going to jump the woman?"

"Don't be stupid." Aden shook his head. "That's not what either of us think. I've gotten to know you. You're a good guy. I just don't want her running or you getting hurt."

Michael scoped the outside sidewalk. Madeline stood under the streetlamp, chatting with Olivia with a huge smile on her face, snow flurries drifting down and glistening like diamonds in her dark hair. "She might be worth the chance."

"Don't say I didn't warn you." Aden opened his door. "Let's go. Olivia's pointing to her watch."

"Yeah, I never said I was a smart man." He waited for Aden to plant the cane and get a steady footing. "And if I recall correctly, I warned you off Shay. How'd that work out?"

"Better than I'd ever dreamed." Aden clapped him on the back. "Good luck, man."

Chapter 5

It took about forty minutes to get to the club.

Olivia had called ahead and spoken to the owner, who graciously reserved them a table near the front.

The early part of the evening was a genuine open mic. It would be after nine before more serious players and singers came out.

Aden snagged a good spot when a car pulled out not far from the entrance.

People milled outside, smoking and talking in small groups under the neon Low Country Public House sign. Jazz brought out a diversity of people, and this place was no different. Older well-to-do's stood chatting with dreadlocked twenty-somethings.

Music was so many things to so many people across time. It could rally people to a cause, or to hate. But at its greatest, music drew people together. It gave hope. It inspired. It comforted.

To Jordan, it was her very heartbeat.

After winding their way through the crowd, Olivia gave their names at the door.

With a curt nod, the gatekeeper let them past.

Aden took Olivia's arm while Michael gripped Jordan's elbow gently. Warmth from his hands radiated through her jacket. Thoughts of those warm hands caused her mind to wander to—*Stop it, Jordan. Focus on the job.*

A moment later, her heart began beating with a different excitement. Not the type caused by fear or anxiety. No, this was the bubbling of anticipation.

The Public House wasn't Jazz House. Grittier, it was like the places found on highways and backroads. Dark, small, and absolutely wonderful. Basic and raw.

Jordan had a feeling someone was going to tear it up tonight. Could she risk singing?

The hostess led them to seats at a small table in the front.

"What can I get for you folks?" A young waitress appeared to take their order.

"I'm driving, so seltzer with lime, please." Aden went first.

The young blonde woman tilted her chin at Olivia. "You, hon?"

"I'd love a glass of cabernet."

"I'll have the same," Jordan chimed in.

The waitress glanced at her, down at her pad, and then up wide-eyed. "Say, you look like that singer."

"Do I? Who?"

"That older gal." She snapped her fingers and a light came on in the woman's eyes. "You look like Sarah Vaughn. Could be her relative. Are you?"

"No, I'm not, but thank you for the wonderful compliment."

"You going to sing something tonight?" The waitress angled her head toward Michael for his order but kept an eye on Jordan while writing down his craft beer choice.

"Not sure." Oh, but she wanted to. "We'll see."

While the woman retrieved the order, Jordan looked around at her table companions. She rolled her eyes at their expectant expressions. "I said, we'll see."

The night progressed. During the changeovers and setups, Michael regaled them with tales ranging from humorous to police work's down and gritty side. He was warm, kind, and funny.

Such a big man, but he seemed to have a gentle spirit, despite what he did for a living. There were some talented performers, but no one caught her attention as a possibility until nearly eleven-thirty.

"Ladies and gentlemen, welcome the CorSam Duo." The MC walked off the stage, and a light shone on the next act.

The drummer, bald and wearing a tight black T-shirt with cutoff sleeves, began a beat under a close spotlight. Another beam revealed a slim woman with coral hair and matching lipstick. She pulled a bow across an electric violin and laid down some sounds on the loop-station on the floor in front of her.

Minutes later, the crowd, including Jordan, were on their feet dancing in place.

When the lights dimmed and the sounds drifted away, she turned to Olivia. "That's what I'm talking about. Let's go find them before they head to another club."

The time flew past.

It was late, almost one a.m., but Jordan was wide awake. Between the fantastic music and great company, she was stoked. Walking out of the club next to Olivia and flanked by the two men, she nearly floated on the chilly air.

The crowd had thinned. Only some smokers getting their fixes.

Jordan held her breath when passing them.

There'd been no opportunity for her to take the stage, which was probably a good thing in hindsight. Instead, they spent time talking to Coral and SammyD, the CorSam Duo. "I have a good feeling about them," she said to Olivia.

"Me too." Olivia squeezed her arm. "You were amazing talking to them. So knowledgeable, especially the floor thing."

"It's called a loop station," Jordan explained. "It plays bits of recorded music, so on stage, it makes it seem like more than Coral played, giving a richer sound to live performances."

"I agree," Michael piped in. "It gave depth to the violin she played."

"You know music?" Jordan glanced up at him. She hadn't made eye contact since he caught her ogling him in the club.

"Strictly amateur." He shook his head and opened the van door.

She slid across the chilly vinyl, and he slipped in after.

Olivia turned and looked over the passenger seat headrest. "They agreed to come by Jazz House late tomorrow morning. SammyD promised to bring a brass-and-wind man named Andre. I'm excited to hear you all together."

Jordan nodded. "I am too. If my instincts are right, we're going to make beautiful music."

They chatted all the way back to Jazz House.

Jordan laughed at the light and friendly teasing between the siblings and Michael. These people were so comfortable to be around. How nice to have friends again.

****

The two women got up and wound their way over to the club owner sitting at the end of the bar.

Michael let out a huge puff of air. A laugh from Aden sitting across the table from him diverted his attentions from his perusal of the beautiful and intriguing woman who'd captivated him. "What's so funny?"

"You are."

There was a knowing smirk on his friend's face. Michael waved a dismissive hand and then picked up his drink. He peeked at the bar where Olivia and Madeline now spoke with the CorSam duo.

There was another burst of hilarity from Aden. "Dude, you've got it bad."

"I've got nothing bad." Muttering, he jiggled a foot.

Aden sat back in the chair with his arms folded. "If you were one of those mutts you care so much about, you'd be panting and drooling."

"My dogs are not mutts." Michael glowered at his best friend. "They're purebred German Shepherds."

"Whatever." Aden tugged his chin toward the bar. "You going to ask her out?"

"What? No. Maybe." He shrugged. "And what are we now, girlfriends?"

"You should."

"Should what? Do your nails?" Michael rolled his eyes. "Besides, it's none of your business."

"Just saying." The other man grinned. "She's been giving you the side-eye all night."

Michael spun to look at the bar. And yup, Madeline's eyes popped wide at being caught in the act of checking him out.

Her attention quickly diverted back to the conversation with the others.

"Told you." Aden snorted.

Michael restrained himself from offering a rude gesture.

The conversation moved on to cars, action movies, and then the revitalization of downtown Slate Quarry and the rising crime rate while keeping half an eye on the women.

"Speaking of"—Aden leaned forward, his expression turning serious.—"have you learned anything else about the Kayla situation?"

"Not really." Michael ran a hand over his head. "My lieutenant isn't talking. He ordered me to keep away from Lane, but I plan to do some investigating on my own time."

Aden took a swig of his seltzer. "I researched Atticus Jones. He's been a restaurant critic for a few years. Before that, he'd worked as a line chef. There's not much more."

"His name is probably a pseudonym." Michael shrugged. "Seems made up. I'll try to get one of my friends at the department to look into him."

"Hey, you boys seem very serious." Olivia scrutinized them. "What're you talking about?"

Instead of answering her, Michael asked, "How'd you make out? Do you have new band members?"

"Yes." Olivia gave a thumbs-up. "Coral and SammyD. They know another guy, so I think we're set. Are you boys ready to go?"

"Yes." Aden caught the waitress's attention and signaled for the check.

While they waited, he and Michael argued over who was paying until Olivia took matters into her own hands and passed her credit card to the barmaid.

A few minutes later, they were outside in the van and heading home.

"Let me drive you home." Michael opened the door to the van when they arrived at the now-dark Jazz House. "It's too late for you to be walking by yourself."

Madeline shook her head. "No. I'll be fine. It's only a few blocks. I'm a big girl who can take care of herself."

"Then let either Aden or me take you." Olivia joined in. "It's after two a.m., and Michael's right."

"Both of you have people you need to get to." Michael crossed his arms over his chest, trying to sound reasonable. "I can see Madeline home."

The woman in question stomped her foot. "Doesn't anyone care what I want?"

Three voices harmonized. "No!"

"Fine, Michael can take me home." She huffed. "I'm sure David is waiting for Olivia, and Shay for Aden."

"Good." Satisfaction filled him. He was dying to get the feisty beauty alone. It was hard to ask for a date with an audience. Placing a hand on her back, he escorted her toward his bluish-green pickup truck. "I'll see you guys around."

After Madeline was belted in the passenger seat, he walked around and climbed in. "What's the address?"

"I really do prefer to walk." Those tawny-brown eyes narrowed at him.

He grinned. "I'll just follow you."

"Tsk, fine." She gave him the address.

He started the vehicle. "I enjoyed myself this evening." He checked the mirrors and pulled out. "The music was great."

She turned and beamed at him. "Yes, it was."

The smile was like a punch in the gut. It took a moment to get a breath. "You had a connection with those people tonight."

"Coral and SammyD are musicians. Most artists connect on some level. Creativity is often the driving force in our lives. It hits somewhere deep." A slim hand with neatly manicured fingers touched her temple. "Here." She lowered her hand to over her stomach. "Here." Her hand moved to her heart. "And here especially." "The head craves the process and culmination of performing and having others enjoy our art. But it's our heart and gut that gets us to put ourselves out there night after night."

Her passion enflamed something in him. Not just desire. Yeah, there was that, but a longing to feel the same way about something. He enjoyed working with the police force. But it wasn't a passion. If he had to leave the job, he could do something else. But what would set him on fire? Besides Madeline Cielo.

A few minutes later, they pulled up in front of a three-story, white house, and he put the vehicle in park.

"Thanks for the ride. I'll be fine from here." The nylon seatbelt whirred back into place. Without even glancing at him, she reached for the door handle.

"Madeline, wait." He reached over and laid a hand on her forearm. "I'd like to see you. Take you to dinner. Maybe even another club."

****

Heat from Michael's palm ran from her arm up

across her chest and into her cheeks. She glanced down at his hand and then slowly up to his earnest face. He was very attractive. But not only that, tonight showed him as funny, caring, and smart. If things were different— *Don't be stupid. No matter what you're feeling, you can't drag this man into the mess of your life.* She steeled her determination. "Michael, I'm sorry. I'm not in a place where dating is even on my radar."

"Please don't say no right off." He slid his hand to grasp hers. "Think about it. No pressure."

With her free hand, she opened the door while extracting her other from his grasp. "No, I won't lead you on. My life is complicated. Thank you for the ride."

The door closing cut off his protest.

She gave him a wave through the window, turned, and walked up to the apartment house without looking back. Once on the other side, she threw the deadbolt and leaned against the wood. A few moments later, she sighed with relief at the sound of the truck pulling away. She pushed off the door and made her way up the long three flights.

On the second-floor landing, a faint meow caught her attention. No pets were the rule, but apartment 2b must have smuggled one in. She smiled, not being above a bit of critter subterfuge herself. Poor Mama never knew what she'd drag home.

The tape in the seam of her door was intact, and she opened it. Everything was in place.

Michael's offer of dinner had almost tempted her into saying yes. She liked him. A lot. More than she should. She glanced at the clock. Two forty-five. Restaurant and club people were night owls, to begin with, but tonight she'd have a hard time going to sleep.

"Okay, tea and a book it is."

Maybe she should sneak a cat in too. As a crazy cat lady, she could talk to it and not feel like she was nuts. In the bathroom, she washed off her makeup and changed. A few moments later, the tea was made, and she grabbed her bag with the books. Reading would take her mind off gentle brown eyes and slightly tousled raven-dark hair.

What would be the harm of a few dates?

Ugh, she wanted to slap herself. Pulling out the first book, she stared at the cover.

A romance with a hunky policeman.

"Are you kidding?" Shoving it to the side, she reached for the second book. It was also a romance, but this one was a western. The cowboy on the front had dark hair. "What was I thinking?" She looked around the empty room. "I definitely need a cat."

The third book in the bag was a cozy mystery with a possible ghost. Perfect.

Three pages in, she set it aside, glanced out of the corner of her eye, and then grabbed the cop romance. A few pages in, all she could think of was Michael and the love scenes.

"Impossible." She spied her composition notebook, where she kept song lyrics and other ideas. Tapping the chewed-up number two pencil, words soon came to her.

There's an ocean of space between us
And across this great divide
My heart aches to be secured
Love's yearning to come alive
If stars could control our destiny
I'm sure they'd let us be

Shining on our love
Blessing you and me

An impossible dream. What she needed was a dose of reality. This situation would not end in a happily ever after. She tapped the pencil against her lips. How could it end? How should it end?

You stand so close, I've only to reach out
But I snatch my hand away
Go out, my love, and find your joy
You must turn away
I must turn away

A tear slid down her cheek, and she threw the notebook across the room.

Chapter 6

"When did you start singing?" Food journalist Mark Ellis from the local paper started with the usual questions.

Jordan smiled at him. Earlier, Olivia had asked her to be part of the interview. She'd initially declined, but in her boss voice, Olivia assured her the terms of the contract about photos would be strictly enforced.

Jordan needed to remain generic. "Growing up in Louisiana, I was immersed in gospel, singing in church and youth groups ever since I was little."

"Who are your influences?" The reporter tapped on the tablet.

"One day, my mom turned the radio to an old jazz-and-blues station." Jordan looked past him, remembering the day she first heard the notes playing. "Once I found them, all the ladies of jazz worked their way into my heart and soul."

Back then she'd stood and stared at the radio where the sounds enraptured her. Now she could scat with the best of them and blended all the greats, creating her own style.

"You remind me of the singer who judged on that TV show." Mark gave her an assessing look.

"I've been told that." Her attention returned to him. Nope, not going to talk about who she looked like.

People liked to compare her to today's popular

singers. But she thought her features more resembled Sarah Vaughan's. There were similarities in the short black hairstyles and arched eyebrows. And the brown eyes, except for the bits of gold in Jordan's. Besides, Sarah was her idol. She was even born on the singer's sixtieth birthday.

"I need to get ready for the show." Jordan stood.

Mark picked up his tablet and stood. "Well, as far as I'm concerned, it looks like you've got a good thing going here. Congratulations. It's going to be a great article." He offered his hand first to Jordan. "Great interview, ladies."

"Thank you. I appreciate your time." Olivia accepted his proffered hand. "If you think this is good, wait a little while for Madeline to take the stage."

I'll hang around and take some pictures." Mark glanced at the stage. "I'll make sure I have permission to use them."

"Please remember to use the photographs provided for Madeline," Olivia repeated the warning from their initial conversation when she agreed to the interview. "I'm bound by contract to her wishes."

"No problem. They're great shots." His nose twitched. "I may order whatever it is that smells so good."

Jordan excused herself and went to the dressing room. In the past, she would've loved the interview. To talk about music was her passion. Too bad all the passion in the world was worthless if you were on the run. She glanced in the mirror as she washed her hands with the lilac-scented soap.

Her mother's soft Louisiana accent whispered in her head. *Make good choices, girl. Make good choices.*

"Sorry, Mama." She spoke to her reflection. "I lost everything with the bad choices. Even you."

If Kyrios knew she was alive, she shook her head. *Don't go down that road.* She lifted the hair from her temple and touched the scar with concealer. "First bad choice I made, Mama."

There was no time for this trip down memory lane. Pulling herself together, she smoothed her hair, once again concealing the scar. Another dab of mascara, then dark-red lipstick, and she was almost ready. Her dress sparkled in the same red as her lipstick. The fringed bottom revealed her long legs. She looked the part.

Madeline Cielo, chanteuse, torch singer, jazz woman. A song riff ran through her mind, but nope, no clown tears in sight. Hidden tears. Not because she was missing a man, but because she'd lost so much. Who she once was, had gone. Jordan had left the building. All that remained—her voice, her pain, and the memories.

The sounds of the band changed to the introduction of her signature song.

Olivia's voice came through the speaker in the ceiling. "Ladies and gentlemen, please welcome to Jazz House stage, Madeline Cielo."

Hands clapped in time to the bass while Jordan strutted to the stage with a broad smile pasted in place. Her red sequined gown shimmered, reflecting the lights.

The band was fantastic. Jazz House scored big, finding them between gigs.

Andre played multiple brass and wind instruments.

Strings were in Coral's lane. Almost anything. If it had strings, she could play.

SammyD put drums through their paces, and Jordan would tickle the ivory as needed.

She began the set with a low, sexy scat. Fingers snapping and shoulders shimmying, she *was* Madeline Cielo.

****

Michael leaned toward the stage. He came to the Jazz House every chance he could. It was tricky with his shifts at the police department. But tonight was his night off. And the woman he fantasized about was on stage. She was sexy and self-assured. Her voice went right through his skin and did funny things to his insides. The few times he'd talked with her, she knocked him out with her smooth, sultry timbre.

"Hey, Michael." Olivia slipped into the seat next to him. "You're back."

"I'm nothing if not persistent." His face warmed while he ran a hand over his short, nearly black hair. Olivia had been nearby when he asked Madeline out for a second time last week and she shot him down. "Besides, this is a great place. You and Shay are doing an amazing job."

"Thanks. I wish everyone thought as you do." Olivia's brown eyes, so similar to his, looked tired and sad. "Can I get you a drink?"

"Seltzer with lime?"

"One of my favorites." Olivia signaled the bartender. "You know you've become part of our life— Aden's and mine. But I know so little about you. You've been in Slate Quarry a long time, right?"

"Screening me, Boss Lady?"

She gave a little laugh. "Suspicious, Mr. Police Officer?"

"Always."

"It's just—well, I already feel like I know you." Olivia peered at him like trying to decipher a puzzle. "I like being able to look into your eyes without seeing myself reflected in those sunglasses you always wear. You're comfortable, like Aden."

"Comfortable is exactly what a man wants to hear from a beautiful woman." He chuckled. "Honestly, there's not much to know. I'm a cop. I have a house on the outskirts of town. My dogs are Jenny and Forest. There're a couple of horses in the barn."

Madeline changed to a torch song, and his attention zeroed back on her. Sitting at the piano now, she sang to her absent lover.

Michael would love to be the one to fill the empty spot if she'd only give him a chance.

"Michael?"

"Yeah?"

"Don't push her. She's shy and very private."

He swung his gaze back to Olivia. "I would never be inappropriate."

"I know. But Madeline is skittish." Olivia sighed. "Give her time to settle in. I don't want to frighten her away. She's important not only to Jazz House but to me."

"Don't worry, Olivia. Scaring her off is the last thing I want to happen."

"Anything new with Kayla?" Olivia's voice wavered, and she touched the side of her head. "How does it work when someone is bailed out?"

"Well, she's out, but there are conditions." He peered at Olivia. She seemed to have it together on the outside, but dark shadows under her eyes when he looked closely were worrisome. She also looked thinner. This wasn't the time to tell her what he'd learned so far. "The judge told her she couldn't have any contact with you, Aden, or Shay. Kayla hasn't reached out, has she?"

"No." Olivia glanced to the side.

"You're not telling me everything. What's going on?" He reached over and laid a hand on hers. "We're friends. You can tell me anything."

She took a deep breath and sat straighter in the chair, pulling her hand away. "Since the—you know—the accident."

"It was an assault. Not an accident." There was a haunted look in her eyes he never saw before. "Olivia, have you talked to anyone since the incident?"

"Of course." Her gaze darted away again. "David, Aden, Shay."

"No, I mean professionally."

Red circles appeared on the woman's cheeks. "I'm fine."

Raising his palms in a sign for peace, he said, "I'm not insinuating you're crazy or anything like that. I've been a police officer for quite a few years. Horrible things happen to people. Good people like you and your brother. It can help to talk to someone. Have you ever heard of PTSD?"

"It's what the soldiers get." She stared down at her hands, twisting in her lap.

"Yes, but not only soldiers." His heart ached for her. She and Aden had become almost like family. He and Aden had gotten off to a rough start a while back when Michael'd been crushing on Shay. But it quickly became obvious those two were made for each other.

He'd backed off but still wasn't sure why he'd latched onto the House twins so easily. "Anyone, under enough stress, can suffer from it."

"I don't know." She lifted her face. "I don't like to think of myself as weak or needy."

"Are soldiers weak?" He leaned forward, peering over his tented hands. "Are victims weak? You're not weak or needy."

She nodded. "I'll think about what you're saying."

"That's all I ask."

"Uh-oh. Set's over." She jumped off the stool. Clapping, she walked to the stage. "Ladies and gentlemen, Madeline and the band will be back after a short break."

He caught Madeline's gaze as she left the room.

****

"How could you—a supposed investigator, and quite expensive—not locate one woman?" Kyrios stared at the man over his cigar. "If my father were alive, you would be pleading for death. It is good you are facing me. I am a modern man and very tolerant. However, you are one more who disappoints me."

Since his youth, Kyrios's dear departed *patéras* not only taught but showed how to maintain control of those around him.

"Kyrie." The investigator's eyes blinked rapidly as he wrung his hands. "Up until three months ago, she was presumed dead."

Since the Lunae Lucem disaster. The final excavation was completed. All the bodies were identified and accounted for. Except one. His wife's. Fury at her deception kindled in his gut, ready to flare up at any provocation. And he was provoked right now.

Patéras, God rest his soul, would beat him within an inch of his life for this tolerance.

The detective agency he hired to find Jordan failed yet again. Perhaps he was too lenient. With renewed resolve, he glared at the man. "Anatole, instruct this *kyon* on how my father, and now I, punished those who fail."

With his hair slicked back and pencil-thin mustache, Anatole looked like the quintessential thug. He stepped forward and grabbed the fool by the back of the neck. "Yes, Kyrie."

The smaller man began to cry while Anatole smiled and dragged him toward the door. "Please, Kyrie. Give me another chance. I will not fail you again."

"I know you won't."

The private investigator's eyes bulged. "Kyrie, no. Please."

Sweat that had been shiny on the man's forehead since he'd walked into the office now ran down the sides of his face in rivulets.

With a wave of dismissal, Kyrios returned to his authentic ebony-wood desk, one of the more-exotic products he illegally traded. "Tito."

The scar-faced bodyguard stepped from the window toward him. "Kyrie? How may I be of assistance?"

"Retrieve all of the information that man had." Kyrios snarled. "And make sure Anatole doesn't screw up."

Tito simply nodded.

When the door shut, he opened the crumpled paper in his hand. How she managed to return to the States, he wasn't sure, but they'd tracked her there. Somehow, she'd arrived there months ago but soon after disappeared—as his mother had attempted but failed.

Rage was too mild to describe his father's emotion. *This is how you deal with faithlessness.* Patéras not only told but showed him when Kyrios was seven years old. His *mitéra* intended to not only leave his father but abandon him—her son. He'd looked on stoically as Patéras disciplined her.

She, too, was American and thought to elude his father. If she'd made it across the ocean, she might have disappeared. Stupid country. People allowed to move where and when they wanted. No law requiring identification for most things. If he had his way, everyone would be like Greece and carry an identity card.

But at the port in Spain, his mother made a fatal mistake by using her passport. His father owned the officials at most ports. It was the only way he could ensure Customs wouldn't interfere in the transfer of the company's "special" products. Trading in things protected by laws around the world, drugs, and occasionally humans, Kyrios continued to build on his father's empire.

Even then, he understood women were trouble. He sympathized with his father. If mitéra made it to the US, who knew what would have happened. Kyrios hated that she chose to leave. Such a disappointment in one who was supposed to love and care for him.

Jordan disappointed him too. What was she until he found her? Nothing. Only a member of a cabaret. He made her a headliner. And how did she repay him? Disrespect.

Enough wallowing. Kyrios crushed the paper into a tight wad and threw it in the wastepaper basket. All this time and expense wasted to find an ungrateful woman. But even though ungrateful, she was his. No one took away what belonged to him.

"Bah." Enough time spent dwelling on Jordan. He pulled the papers detailing the proposal to the US officials from the top drawer and lit another cigar. Now he would infiltrate the business community, starting in Philadelphia. After all, that was the city his dear mitéra came from.

Kyrios slammed the intercom button. "Get me the Philadelphia team."

Chapter 7

In the empty dressing room, Jordan leaned in to touch up her makeup.

Michael was back.

She noticed him at the bar during her first set, talking to Olivia.

Excitement had tickled her stomach the previous week when he asked her to dinner. She was too rattled the first time she saw him to notice much more than the uniform. Since the night they went to the club, he'd been by Jazz House several times, including the past week when he'd asked her out again.

So handsome.

Dark, almost-black hair was short on the sides and not too long on top. It was adorable how he ran a hand through it and mussed it when he asked her for a date. When he'd pulled off the mirrored aviator glasses, his brown eyes, bracketed with laugh-lines, made her want to melt. She always liked a big man, and he certainly fit the bill—tall, broad across the shoulders, with a trim waist. The man filled out a pair of jeans.

Turning him down was hard, but for the best. Right now was no time for a relationship. Plus, she was a fraud. It was hard enough lying during work hours, but at home too? No way. She pushed aside the thoughts. Break was over, and the band had begun her intro. She snapped her bag closed, took a deep breath, and walked back to the stage.

She scanned the crowd. Oh, Michael now sat at the table closest to the platform. She shook off the jitters and warmed up with a familiar jazz standard. He seemed focused and listening to the words of bewildered bewitchment. It was an appropriate song. He was truly capable of putting a spell on her.

The night flew by, and soon it was down to the closing. The next song on the playlist about star-crossed lovers, she wrote herself. A few bars into the torch song, she couldn't help singing directly to him.

"There's an ocean of space between us."

She should never have started this. Her hand went to her heart as a catch caught in her throat, and she stumbled over the next words.

"If stars could control our destiny. I'm sure they'd let us be."

The room became hushed. Even the clatter of cutlery and murmuring from the diners ceased.

"Now is not the time or place." Her voice cracked. *"So, I must go away."*

Unable to maintain eye contact as she continued, she lowered her gaze and stared at her red shoes. When she lifted her head, Michael's normally boyish easygoing expression was gone, and in its place, a pensive man stared at her.

"You stand so close, I've only to reach out." Her hand, almost of its own accord, stretched toward him. *"But I snatch my hand away. Go out, my love, and find your joy."*

For a moment, it appeared he was going to get up and come to her.

In song, she pleaded. *"You must turn away. I must*

turn away."

The spotlight faded with the notes as a red gel backlit the stage.

She brushed away the tears running down her cheeks before the stage lights came back up.

The room was silent until someone began to clap, then the audience burst into applause.

By the time the stage brightened, Jordan had painted on her practiced smile once again. "Thank you."

Two more. She only had to get through two more songs before she could go home. Only then would she allow herself to have a meltdown—where no one would know. It wasn't precisely Michael who caused the despondence filling her because she didn't know him well enough. But it was the possibilities he represented—someone to love, and a family to call her own. Something inside told her if the circumstances were different, given time, they could be happy together.

SammyD began counting the beat to the next song with his sticks.

You're a professional, Jordan. Get it together.

And she did.

A few minutes later, Olivia joined her on the stage. "Ladies and gentlemen, thank you for joining us this evening. How about another round of applause for Madeline Cielo and the band."

Clapping continued while she left the stage and headed back to the dressing room.

"Why, Madeline?"

Michael's voice stopped her from turning the doorknob. "Why, what?" She couldn't turn and face him.

"The song. Why must I turn away?" Michael didn't touch her, but she could feel his warmth right behind her. "Why must you? From the moment we met, there was something between us. Not just from my side."

"No, Michael, it's just from your side." Jordan dug deep for strength. She had to put him off, no matter what. He was a cop. With her background, he would dig and dig. There was no way she could put not only him, but the House family in danger. She turned around and pulled her shoulders back. "You're a nice guy, but that's all."

"You sang to me tonight." He looked unsure now.

Guilt stung at what she needed to do. "Tsk, it's a show. Just a show. I make contact with someone. It draws emotion from people. I'm sorry if you thought it was more. Goodnight."

Reaching behind her, she turned the doorknob and slipped through. She closed it firmly and leaned against it.

"Goodnight, Madeline." Michael spoke from the other side. "I'm sorry if I bothered you."

His steps faded away, and she walked to the mirror. While taking off her makeup, she wondered again what could have been between them if allowed to grow.

A few minutes later, someone tapped on the door.

"Yes?"

"Madeline, can I come in?" It was Olivia.

"Of course."

The other woman's brown eyes, which were so much like Michael's, caught her gaze in the mirror. "Are you all right? I know Michael followed you back."

"I'm fine. He had unrealistic expectations for us.

We're straight now."

"Ok." Olivia bit her lip and looked like she wanted to say more.

Jordan cut her off. "I'm here to sing. Work. I've no time for nor want a relationship."

"Right." Olivia nodded. "But, Madeline, if you ever need someone to talk to, I'm here."

There was another rap at the door.

"We good to come in?" Coral called.

"Yes," Jordan answered, heading off any further personal discussion.

"We had a great night," Olivia told the group when they filed in and milled about. "Thank you all very much."

Jordan glanced back at the mirror and wiped the rest of her makeup off while they all said goodnight. When she looked up, Olivia was gone, too, and the door into the hallway stood open like a black maw waiting to devour her. She shook off the morbid idea and walked through it.

Only a few people were left finishing drinks at the bar. The staff bustled around the tables, cleaning up.

Michael was gone.

****

Michael slammed the truck's door while standing in the driveway of his cabin-style house. He was such an idiot. Why was he always attracted to women who wanted nothing to do with him?

Loud, excited barking came from inside.

Scrubbing his face with his palms, he muttered, "Take it easy. I'm coming."

Even to his own ears, he sounded pathetic. *Get a grip, man.*

The lock clicked after he plugged in the code. When he opened the door, one-hundred-fifty pounds of solid muscle and fur nearly knocked him over. "Geez, guys. I was only gone a couple of hours."

Apparently, a few hours were the same as a lifetime.

He sat on the porch steps and submitted to a face washing, sniff down, and occasional whack in the head by a German Shepherd tail. Nothing could be better, in his book, except maybe a woman on the step beside him. *Sap.* When Forest tried to tackle him down, he had enough. "Let's go watch some TV."

Jenny yipped her agreement to the plan, and the two nearly knocked him over again. By the time he changed into track shorts and a T-shirt, the two couch potatoes had claimed their spots. Michael grabbed a bottle of water and flopped onto the brown leather recliner, which matched the sofa. Nothing good was on, so he flipped on the news.

National news was no news. Political griping and catcalling reached a new level of ridiculousness.

In his opinion, both sides needed to reel it in.

"Whatever happened to respect and courtesy?" he asked Forest. The only reply was a snore. "What do you think, J?"

Jenny jumped off the couch, padded over, and laid her head on his knee.

Michael stroked her soft fur. "Well, you're the only female to give me the time of day."

In other news, the anchorman droned on. *The business community is buzzing. Plans are in development with billionaire Greek tycoon Kyrios Vasilakis. Later this year, Vasilakis intends to visit*

Philadelphia to discuss opening a U.S. arm of his vast array of companies…

Michael yawned and clicked off the television. "Come on, you two. Let's go out one last time and then to bed."

A jacket hung on a peg by the backdoor slider above his slip-on boots. Even though the yard was fenced, he liked to go out with the Shepherds after dark. Plus, the fresh air might clear his head.

The dogs ran down into the backyard.

Michael rolled his eyes. Finding the perfect spot could take a few minutes, so he leaned against the deck.

It was a nice night. Clear. Stars twinkled, and the Big Dipper stood out against the inky space.

He traced the two bowls with his finger and then tracked to the North Star and over to the Little Dipper's handle.

Everyone thought because he was a cop, he was a big tough guy. He could be when needed, but his mom once told him he had a poet's heart. When she died, it left a big hole in his life. He never knew his father. No brothers or sisters. Just him and mom. It's why he liked being on the police force. First Responders became a surrogate family.

That way, in his loneliness, he wasn't alone. Not that anyone knew. He was never the party guy or the funny guy. He was the guy you called when you needed something and then forgot about. Yeah, he showed up at department functions but mostly remained in the background. "Geez, I'm wallowing."

Forest and Jenny barking near the fence at the back of the property kept him from punching himself in the face.

"That's it." He whistled, and they came running. "All right, bed."

He'd spent enough time hosting his own pity party. The hounds raced upstairs, but the laptop caught his attention. He grabbed a glass of iced tea from the fridge while it woke up.

Settling in, he stared at the screen, then typed in Atticus Jones. An hour later, his eyes burned, and a yawn escaped. Nothing. The guy seemed to come out of nowhere.

Michael scrubbed his face. What about the only other link to Jones? That diner where the guy'd worked prior to doing the Restaurant Auditor blog. He opened the history bar and clicked on Downtown Eats. There was a picture of the staff surrounding the owner in a dining room. Michael located Jones and tilted his head as he read the caption.

Listed from left to right were the employee names: Ernesto Fernandez, Lucas Albertson, owner Oscar Washington, and Arthur Brandt. And he looked exactly like a younger version of the Restaurant Auditor blog's author.

Michael sat back and studied the picture before searching for Arthur Brandt. There was an old social media page. Bingo! He was the cousin of none other than Detective Oliver Brandt, formerly of Slate Quarry Police Department.

A loud breath of air escaped Michael. Brandt had quit the department after being linked to Kayla Lane and her crimes. Nothing stuck to him regarding Lane's actual violations, but he refused suspension over how he'd handled the case and Shay.

Why would a cop's cousin shell out ten thousand

dollars? It was going to be a long night. It was almost three in the morning. He'd hit a dead end with Kayla Lane's connection to the Brandt cousins. The Brandts, except for one picture on the outdated social media site, didn't appear close. But no way was this a coincidence.

Michael stood and stretched.

Except for the hum of the refrigerator motor, the only other sound was the oil burner turning the heat on.

Passing through the house toward his bedroom, he flipped off the lights.

Hoping he'd tired himself out enough to sleep, Michael shoved the dogs over, climbed into bed, and lay down with his arms crossed behind his head. He stared at the ceiling. The night light from the bathroom illuminated the room enough to see once his eyes adjusted.

Past choices and decisions clash with the wishes of today. Now is not the time or place. So I must go away.

The song and look on Madeline's face as she sang were imprinted on his mind and in his heart. There was truth in her voice as she performed. But what choices? And more importantly, what wishes?

More of the song drifted through him as his eyes fluttered shut.

Chapter 8

Jordan sat on the side of her bed. Her heart pounded violently as she stared at the phone. She always thought when the time came, she'd be able to think logically and create a plan, but her mind remained blank except for one thought.

Kyrios was coming.

At first, when the phone vibrated with the news alert, she thought she was still dreaming. But now, with sleep in the rearview mirror, she knew it was a nightmare—a waking one. She scrolled down the page.

Billionaire Greek tycoon Kyrios Vasilakis is to arrive in Philadelphia, Pennsylvania, later this month. Sources say he has been in discussions with the Commerce Department about opening a U.S. arm of his vast array of companies...

Tears blurred the rest of it.

"Move, Jordan." She scrambled across the cold floor to the closet and grabbed her black duffel go-bag from the floor. It stuck on something. She yanked frantically. "Come on. Come on."

The bag suddenly released, and she fell flat on her back with the wind knocked out of her. Focusing on a crack in the ceiling, she tried to slow her breathing. "You're okay. He's not here." Tears flowed out of the corner of her eyes. "There's time."

After a few more deep breaths, she dashed away

the tears tickling her ears where they'd pooled. She sat up and hugged her knees while rocking back and forth.

Philadelphia was a long way from Slate Quarry. Kyrios didn't know she was alive, much less living in Pennsylvania."

She crawled back to the side of the bed, where she'd dropped her phone. Turning, she leaned against the frame and woke the cell back up.

A Vasilakis representative told the reporters at the press conference that Vasilakis Enterprises has been looking for a port in the US for several years. Since the dredging of the Delaware River, Philadelphia has become a viable option for the Greek magnate's ships. Mr. Vasilakis will now join the ongoing discussions stateside and meet with the mayor and business leaders in the community.

"Okay, okay. It's nothing new." If the discussion had been going on for years, then it was only a coincidence."

There were several other stories in her alerts. A popular online celebrity rag's headline read,

Kyrios Vasilakis, Greece's most eligible bachelor, is coming to the States.

Jordan tapped to open the story.

Since the tragic death of his wife, Jordan, a year ago, the Greek billionaire has not been a lonely widower. Vasilakis seems to have been filling the void left by his wife quite well. Seen regularly on the arms of European starlets and models, the Greek playboy appears to have recovered from the loss.

"Ugh." He probably had plenty of those even when she lived in Greece.

She scrolled to the next story. A crime/mystery

blog had followed Kyrios for years. The writer claimed Jordan's husband was a crime lord, and the person was suspicious of the circumstances regarding her death.

With so many jumping aboard the Kyrios Vasilakis business deal, it is my journalistic duty to warn the public. Many mysteries surround the alleged underground syndicate leader from Greece.

The columnist listed many of Kyrios's suspected ties and dealings with criminals. Still, he ended with one that touched home with her.

And lastly, do not forget the beautiful and talented American singer Jordan Welles, who went missing during an assault at one of Vasilakis' clubs. There were many casualties and fatalities, from not only the shooting, but due to the fire from an incendiary device that burned long and hot. Could it be a coincidence that Ms. Welles-Vasilakis' body was the only one authorities never recovered?

What did Kyrios think? Did he assume her remains were gone to ash? She'd seen pictures of the fire. The club had been leveled. Or did he believe the enemy took her out? The only other choice was that she had run.

Sweat trickled down her spine.

Laying her head back, she looked up at the ceiling and sent up a silent prayer for guidance. She dropped the phone when it rang and vibrated, scaring her to death. Snatching it from the floor next to her, she looked at the screen. *Michael.* She looked back toward the ceiling with a raised eyebrow. "Really?"

****

After a night of tossing and turning, but mostly spent with thoughts of Madeline and trying to figure out the connection between them, Michael came to the conclusion things weren't what they seemed on the surface. There was something in her eyes when she rejected him. Fear.

Being a cop for so long gave him an almost sixth sense with most people. Their body language at times was nearly as loud as the words. The way Madeline kept glancing away revealed practically as much as when she held his gaze. She was attracted to him, but hiding something. Was she married? Hiding from an ex? Could she be a criminal?

He bolted up and sat on the edge of the bed.

Jenny opened one eye, closed it, and went back to sleep.

Michael glanced over toward the door.

Forest sat there panting and eyeing him.

"Give me a minute, will you?" He got up and went into the attached bathroom. He finished up at the sink and looked at his reflection. "Nah, it couldn't be."

No, it wasn't the criminal kind of fear of the law. Something haunted this woman. The way she scanned the areas before she got out of the vehicle. How she'd jumped at a dropped tray at the club they'd visited. Was she abused?"

"All right, let's go, Jenny."

The German Shepherd wagged her tail but didn't bat an eye.

Forest made a quick exit when he opened the bedroom door, and Jenny flopped over onto her side.

"Fine, no breakfast for you."

She nearly plowed him over in the doorway.

"Can't feed you if you kill me," he muttered but smiled and followed the two furry beasts downstairs.

While they were out in the yard, he made a pot of coffee and fixed their breakfast.

A yip at the door alerted him the hounds were back and hungry. He opened the door and stepped to the side, then shook his head at them scrambling for traction on the tile. "You act like I starve you."

The coffee finished with a gurgle and hiss.

He poured a cup and inhaled the rich nutty scent before sitting and gazing out into the backyard. Madeline was a mystery. One he wanted to solve. He couldn't push her into something she wasn't willing to give. He hesitated. The woman seemed pretty adamant in her brush-off.

Memories of how waiting for the right moment with Shay had left him in the cold when first Nick, and then Aden came into her life. He'd thought for a long time he loved her. Now he realized it hadn't been love, but the desire to have someone by his side he cared about.

He stared over the rim of his *proudly owned by German Shepherds* mug. Subliminally had he waited because she wasn't the one? Or was it fear of rejection when he delayed his intentions?

Michael ran a hand over his hair. Before Shay, there had been two other women, but he'd waited with them as well. Hearing his mom cry over his missing dad at night when she thought he was asleep still made him sad.

Grow up, man. You're not your mom.

He dialed the phone.

"Hello," she answered on the third ring.

"Hi, it's Michael."

"I know. Your name came up."

"Is everything okay? You sound upset."

"I'm all right." She sniffled. "What can I do for you?"

He hesitated and then got up and began to pace, coffee cup in one hand and phone in the other. *You've got to get this right.*

"Michael?"

"Yeah, I'm here." He stopped and leaned against the back-door jamb. "Listen, I know you said no. But I'm hoping you'll reconsider."

"Look, Michael"—her voice was soft and hesitant on the other side—"there're things. Stuff I can't talk about. I can't do a romantic relationship right now, but I really could use a friend."

"How about this. We go slow. Get to know each other. No pressure." He let out a deep breath. "But let's see where it goes without closing the door on—more. I won't lie. I'm attracted to you. And I'm pretty sure you are to me."

"I don't know."

"Meet me for coffee. I promise I won't push or try to force information you don't want to give."

Through the phone, he heard a siren. Typical downtown noise let him know she hadn't hung up. *Be patient.* His jaw ached from clenching it while waiting for an answer.

"Okay."

A smile erupted on his face. He reached down and ruffled Jenny's ears. "Okay."

****

Pull yourself together, girlfriend. With her heart fighting her head, Jordan's stomach twisted into knots. She was torn about meeting Michael. Loneliness was a terrible thing. For so long, she'd been surrounded by people but had no one to confide in. No one to hold her. No one to share joys or troubles with.

The water took forever to turn tepid. She'd learned to deal with the old building's plumbing, but it still wasn't fun to take a cold shower. When the lackluster stream turned reasonably warm, she stepped into the tub.

After toweling off quickly, she slipped into her robe and slippers then went to the ancient armoire and riffled through her wardrobe. Only the fact she shopped at consignment stores and was talented with a needle and thread meant she had a decent selection of not only casual clothes, but performance dresses that were top-notch.

The midnight-blue sweater with silver thread went well with her jeans. She chose a pair of chunky boots to finish the ensemble. *Always dress to impress.* But who was she trying to impress? *Michael, that's who.*

"You are crazy." She pointed at her reflection. How could she be with him? Not only would she be putting him in danger, but he was a cop. In this case, her heart trumped logic. "In for a penny."

After she rolled her eyes at herself, she grabbed her hat, coat, and purse. If she didn't leave now, she'd chicken out. And she really didn't want to chicken out. Outside on the stoop, she scanned the area. Nobody suspicious. She took off down the street at a quick clip. The Heavenly Brew coffee house was only a few minutes' walk away from her apartment. If she hurried, she'd beat him there. It would give her a chance to settle in and maybe look calm and collected.

Friends, they'd agreed. But how could it work

when she was so attracted to him? Looking both ways, she began to cross the street.

Beep!

A white sedan came speeding through the light, and she jumped back.

"Hey!" Did that guy just give her the one-finger salute? "You're so rude," she yelled after the car.

"I don't think he heard you."

Jordan glanced over at the blonde now standing next to her. "Probably not. But hollering at him made me feel better."

"I know what you mean." She shrugged and smiled up at Jordan. "My name's Hailey. You live around here?"

"I'm Madeline." Not really free with information, but her mother taught her to be polite. "Yes, I have an apartment nearby. You?"

"Come on, let's cross before the light changes." Hailey stepped off the curb. "I live up over the bakery on the next block."

"That would make me gain fifty pounds." Jordan jumped over a puddle.

"I bet you can sing." Hailey stepped up onto the opposite sidewalk and turned to face Jordan with her hands on her hips. "You can? Right?"

"You think I can sing?" Jordan skirted a lump of unnamed slush in the gutter. "Why?"

"Because of the tone, timbre, and texture of your talking voice." Hailey adjusted her backpack.

"Are you a musician?" Jordan turned to face the smaller woman.

"Sort of." She popped her gum. "I went to school for music. I want to be a producer and engineer."

"That's so great." Jordan was impressed. "We need more women on the technical side of the industry. And yes, I do sing. I'm working at Jazz House."

"The new restaurant? I've been meaning to check it out." Hailey glanced at her phone. "Oops, I've got to go. Class starts soon. Maybe I'll see you around."

"Maybe." She watched the younger woman jog off while adjusting her tie-dyed backpack, then continued toward the coffee shop. Meeting and talking to new people was a joy after being on her own and alone for so long. This town was the kind of place you could put roots down in.

Speaking of putting down roots, Michael was the kind of man to do that with. *Stop it, Jordan. It's not going to happen.* What was she thinking, accepting a coffee date with him? She crossed the next street and peered into the consignment-store window. Several of the dresses hanging had great potential, and there was a pair of silver shoes to die for. The shop was closed, but she might have time to stop in tomorrow.

Moments later, after calculating her cash-flow situation and what she could spend on clothes after breakfast, she arrived at Heavenly Brew. Scents of coffee and cinnamon wafted out on the warm air from inside as she held the door open to let an older man and woman exit.

They smiled and thanked her.

There. An empty table by the big front window. She peeled off her hat and gloves and shoved them into a pocket. Then she hung her coat on the back of the bistro chair and sat to people watch.

The diversity of patrons was typical for a coffee house. College kids on their phones or laptops sat near a group of laughing women discussing a familiar best-seller. Moms with strollers sat by the back wall, out of the way, obviously enjoying some grown-up time. Businesspeople waited in the take-out line.

"Can I get you something?" a red-headed waiter with a green Heavenly Brew apron asked.

The whimsical logo, a coffee cup with wings and a halo, tickled her. "I'm waiting for someone. Can you give me a minute?"

"Sure. I'll come back." He laid two paper menus on the table and went to the next customer.

With her chin propped in her hand, Jordan stared out the window at snow flurries drifting past on the wind. Her tummy did a somersault when Michael pulled up across the street in his pickup.

He looked both ways and lifted a hand of thanks to a driver who stopped for him. Handsome features became clearer when he pulled off his aviator sunglasses, hooked them in his collar, and jogged over.

His rosy cheeks were as endearing as the tousled, almost-black hair cut shorter on the sides. She itched to run her hand through the longer top with its hint of curls.

Spotting her, he flashed a smile of straight white teeth.

Oh, good grief, was that a dimple?

A few of the moms, and most of the ladies' book club, turned to ogle him when he came through the door.

But he only had eyes for her.

Michael yanked his gloves off and slipped out of a navy peacoat. His long-sleeved black T-shirt hugged his muscular torso and arms. The matching jeans did the same to his legs and tush.

Jordan's heart sped up, and if she were a southern belle, she might have swooned.

"Madeline. I'm so glad you said yes." He pulled out the chair opposite her. "Have you been waiting long?"

"No, only a few minutes." When he called her Madeline, it startled her out of a fantasy of what his lips might taste like. Any relationship they had, whether friends or more, would be based on lies. She *so* wanted to find out where this could go. But how much could she reveal?

If Michael ever found out, could he trust her again? Forgive her?

Chapter 9

What the heck? The look on her face when he said her name wasn't really shock. But surprise? Definitely.

He didn't say anything. This woman had secrets, but he was confident she'd come clean eventually. He was just going to be happy with the fact she'd changed her mind about going out with him, even if only for coffee and friendship.

The waiter came over. "Hey, Officer Machau. Almost didn't recognize you dressed as real people. You want your usual Jersey sandwich?"

"What's a Jersey sandwich?" Madeline perused the menu. "I don't see it here."

"You won't see it called that on the menu." Michael smiled over at her. "And the great debate depends on whether you're from North or South Jersey."

"A great debate?" She lifted an eyebrow at him. "Over a breakfast sandwich and while in Pennsylvania?"

"We get a lot of Jersey folks over here." The waiter nodded. "By the way, you can search it on the web."

"What is this mystery item?"

"Taylor, egg, and cheese," Michael answered.

Now the waiter was shaking his head. "Nope. Pork roll, egg, and cheese."

Two old guys sitting at the next table heard them

and began to argue too.

"Taylor."

"Nope, it's pork roll."

"See," Michael thumbed over his shoulder. "Great debate even here in Pennsylvania. And don't even get them started on scrapple."

"Okay." She laughed. "I'll have to try this Jersey sandwich and see what all the fuss is about. I'll take a coffee and orange juice as well."

"You got it." The waiter jotted the order down then looked at him. "Coffee and OJ?"

He could only nod because her laughter took his breath away. Low and husky, it reminded him of sultry nights, good music, and a ruby-red glass of wine. Their eyes met across the table, and she held the gaze for a few seconds before turning to stare out the window. "Friends? Right?"

A small smile appeared, and she looked back. "Friends."

"Good. Now, as friends, I should know a little more about you."

She stiffened.

"And you should know more about me."

Her shoulders relaxed. "Where do you live?"

Okay, so he was going first. "I have a piece of property outside of town. It's a decent-size house which I share with Forest and Jenny.

"Forest and Jenny?" Her head tilted to the side, and she did an Elvis lip. "Who are they?"

"Not imaginary friends." He snorted. "German Shepherds who adopted me a few years ago. There's a barn out back where two fat and sassy horses live as well."

"Adopted you?"

"Yep. I responded to a hoarding situation." He frowned, remembering the scene. "An older couple. Their situation had gotten out of control. There were no family or friends to help."

"I've seen that television show about hoarding and wondered how such a thing happens to people."

"Sneaks up on them." He smiled and nodded at the waiter setting their breakfast down. "Thanks."

Madeline looked at the massive sandwich in front of her and raised an eyebrow. "Great debate, huh?"

"You'll see."

She pressed it down, cut it in half, then took a bite and moaned. "That's delicious."

"Jersey sandwich." He took a bite and explained about the hoarders. "They had a bunch of dogs. In their mind, they were rescuing them. Saving them. But it wasn't good for either the dogs or them."

"And Forest and Jenny were part of it?"

"Yeah, they were young. Not puppies. Sort of teenagers. Skinny with patches of fur missing. But something about them touched me." He choked up. "Especially, when after all they'd been through, they licked my hand through the wire of the crate."

Madeline reached over and laid her hand on his. "You're a good man, Michael."

Before Michael could cover it with his other hand, she pulled hers back. How was he going to keep his distance from this woman?

She pulled the paper wrapper from the straw and twirled it with her fingers, glancing up through her lashes.

"It's okay." His shoulders drooped a little. "We

said friends."

Jordan nodded. "Just friends."

They chatted about a little of everything over their breakfast, from books to music and movies. Much of their tastes were similar. Though she liked the ones who guarded the galaxy and he the man dressed in an iron suit, they both agreed their creator was a genius.

They finished eating and were sipping their coffee when Madeline sighed.

"What's wrong?"

After setting down her cup, she leaned forward and reached across the table, and laid her hand on his.

"If we were…more"—her leg started bouncing under the table—"would you have to ask a lot of questions about my past? Or could we pretend my life began when I moved to Slate Quarry?"

He gently turned her hand over. "I can wait until you're ready to tell me."

"What if I'm never ready?"

The smile faded from his lips, and a frown drew his brows down. "I only have to know you're not like a— wanted criminal."

"No. It's nothing like that." Her eyes went wide at his idea she was a criminal.

A goofy half-grin broke across his face. "My lieutenant wouldn't like it."

"How about an answer? What if I can never tell you?"

He leaned back in the chair, stretching to keep hold of her hand. Staring her straight in the eyes, he took a deep breath, let it out. Then a tight nod of his head. "I promise I will never push you for information about your past. I hope with time, you'll learn to trust me. But

I need a promise too."

"What kind of promise?" Madeline drew her bottom lip between her teeth.

"Promise me, if you're ever in trouble or danger, you'll let me help." Michael leaned toward her and cupped her cheek over the remains of their breakfast. "I need your word you won't bail without giving me a chance to stand beside and support you."

Tears welled in her eyes. She gave him a shaky nod.

"No, Madeline. I need words."

"I promise."

The words, soft and tremulous, nearly broke his heart. Michael sat straight and picked up the bill. "What do you say we go meet my menagerie."

"Oh, Michael. I'd love to meet them." Jordan stood and brushed a few crumbs off her shirt. "I just need to run to the ladies' room."

****

In the restroom, she locked the door, went straight to the sink, and stared at the mirror. She raised her hand to her warm cheek. "What have you done?"

A shiny-eyed woman looked back at her. *It will be all right.*

He said he wouldn't push for information.

Mama's voice came to her. *Make good choices.*

Was this a good choice? She sure hoped so.

When she returned to the front, Michael was paying the bill.

"Hey, you don't have to pay the whole thing." She fumbled for her wallet.

"Stop. I don't have to." He put a generous tip in the jar next to the register. "I want to."

After crossing the street, he opened the door to the truck. "Hope you don't mind dog hair."

"Nope." She climbed in and buckled up. "I love dogs."

The dimple reappeared. "Good. And they're going to love you."

Michael shut the door and skirted around the tailgate. He climbed in, and a minute later, they were on their way.

"Don't you have to work today?" Jordan asked during the drive. "I don't have to be at Jazz House until this evening."

"Not today. We have rotating schedules. I don't go back to work until tomorrow night." He opened the console and pulled out a roll of cherry ring-shaped candies. "Want one?"

"Mmm, my favorite flavor."

He flipped one up with his thumb.

She reached across the console. Static electricity snapped when she took it. Yep, they had a charge between them. She popped it into her mouth.

Even though it was still winter, the pale sun was able to warm the day. It shone through the evergreens, which gave a splash of color against the bare limbs of the maple and oak trees.

She snuck in a quick glance away from the passing scenery to her driver. It was hard to keep from looking at him.

About ten minutes later, he slowed down and pointed. "That's my house."

Michael turned into the driveway where a smallish log cabin, set back from the road, stood nestled in the trees. The Pocono Mountains behind it lent a Norman

Rockwell feel.

Fence rails ran the length of the wooded lot, and she spotted a small barn near the back where two russet-red horses grazed.

"It's only a couple of acres, but it's all mine." He shrugged and parked the truck.

"I love it." She smiled over at him. "It fits you."

"Thanks. Wait and let me get the door." Not pausing for her to reply, he jumped out of the vehicle and trotted to her side.

Jordan unclicked her seat belt and turned. "I could've opened it myself."

"I know, but I wanted to do it." Michael glanced toward the house where barking and whining emitted. "Are you sure you're ready for this? They can be a bit much when meeting new people."

"Bring them on." Jordan rubbed her hands together. "I'm a dog person and haven't had my arms around one for ages."

A big hand enveloped hers, and he led the way to the porch. "Sit in the chair, or else they'll knock you over in their excitement."

Two lovely dark-stained wooden rocking chairs flanked a matching table.

Jordan smiled and began to rock back and forth. "I could get used to country living."

Michael shot her a piercing look. "That's what I'm hoping."

"Michael."

"No." He lifted his hand. "Sorry. I promised to go slow."

"Well, you're going slow—slow letting those fur babies out here."

"All right. All right." His smile returned. "Just remember. You asked for this."

A big black nose smeared the window next to the door. Then another one, a bit smaller, appeared.

Michael stooped down and nearly pressed his nose to the opposite side. "Behave yourselves. Don't make me look bad."

After a twist of the doorknob, he scrambled to slow them down. Nope, not even close.

Jordan slid off the chair and onto the porch floor. Wriggling, squiggling bodies nearly covered hers. She grinned up through the ever-moving fur, ears, tails, and noses. "You're all so gorgeous."

"Me too?" He propped a hip on the railing and leaned against the post.

"Yes, you too." She buried her warming face in the dogs' scruff.

The dogs settled down. Forest went belly up for a tummy rub while Jenny tried to be a lap dog, failing miserably.

After a while of rotating who got a belly rub and who got scratched behind the ears, Jordan shivered when the sun went behind a cloud.

****

"Want to come in? He stood and offered a hand. It felt right when Madeline took it and he pulled her to her feet. "I'll light a fire and make some hot chocolate."

She walked in beside him. "Oh, Michael. I love it. It's like a cabin you'd see on television."

"You investigate while I go make the cocoa."

"Here you go." He walked in with a tray holding two steaming stoneware mugs and a plate of shortbread cookies.

"I love your house." Jordan sat on one end of the soft, brown sofa. "It's so cozy."

"Thanks." He sat on the other side and then grabbed a cup, blew, and took a sip. "I told the architect what I wanted—from the paneled wall to the beamed ceiling."

"The fireplace is huge."

"The stones were quarried not far from here." A warmth that had nothing to do with the fireplace spread through his chest at her admiration. "The beams were reclaimed from a barn someone was going to tear down and get rid of."

They petted the dogs and talked comfortably for hours. Even the few silences weren't awkward.

Italian was a mutual favorite food. Vacations at the beach were a must.

Michael's brows lifted when she surprised him by saying she liked to fish and wasn't opposed to camping. "Really?" He scratched Jenny behind the ears. "You seem like a city girl."

She tossed her head. "I, sir, am a modern woman."

They laughed, and she told him about a disastrous camping trip as a kid. "It rained constantly. The tent leaked, and all we heard was people in a nearby tent yelling *Yahtzee* all day and night."

Before he knew it, it was nearing the time to go to Jazz House, but he didn't want to be alone again. He picked up the now-empty tray. "Do you mind if I stay and listen?"

"Aren't you tired of me yet?"

"Nah. We've just started getting to know each other."

"I know a way we can get better acquainted." She

scooched over closer.

"H-h..." He cleared his throat. "How?"

Jordan sat facing him cross-legged. With her chin propped in her hands, she blinked owl-eyes at him. "You could kiss me."

"Really?" His head tilted to the side. "What about taking it slow?" He searched her eyes and grasped one of her hands. "I'm trying to understand what's happening here, Madeline. You were so adamant about taking time and not moving forward into a relationship."

Sitting back on her heels, she tried to retract her hand, looking unsure and wavering at his words.

But Michael covered her hand with his and wouldn't let go. He pressed his cheek into it. "Talk to me. Tell me what's going through your head. I don't want you to regret today."

Closing her eyes, she took a deep breath. "I've been alone for a long time. I have trust issues, but I want to trust you. I like you a lot."

"We can reel this back." He didn't want to. For years he'd searched for her not even knowing. With all her secrets and mystery—it was this woman. And he wanted to kiss her like he needed air to breathe.

****

Those simple words caused her heart to stutter. "No. I don't want to. I want your arms around me. I want you to kiss me."

He's right. What are you doing?

Heat ran from Jordan's chest up to her neck and flooded her cheeks. What was she doing? Her mind screamed, *Stop!* But it was her heart she listened to. A heart that wanted to be held and treasured for at least a little while. A heart that had been beaten down and made to feel worthless. Now it flared back to life, reminding her of the woman she once was. The woman she could become. One in control of her life and destiny. Free to make her own choices. And she wanted to choose Michael.

She slid across the brown leather and knelt facing him. Butterflies fluttered in her stomach. She searched his face while she struggled to find the right words. Here was a man she could love. One who would maybe cherish her the way she needed.

Michael's expression tore at her heart. The mixed signals she was sending had to be frustrating.

He reached over, grasped her waist, and pulled her into his lap.

Jordan wound her arms around his neck, and she gazed into his eyes. She licked her lips. The scent of chocolate and sugar drifted on his breath.

Michael cupped her cheek and waited.

A short inhalation hitched, and she pulled him toward her. Tipping her head to the side, she closed the distance and lightly rubbed her lips against his. After a few tentative kisses later, she leaned away.

He waited, not rushing her.

A groan escaped him when she pulled him to her once again. He smelled like chocolate cherries and winter. She explored his lips with hers. Lightly caressing and tasting.

Michael's arm wound tighter around her waist, and he cupped the back of her head. When she didn't pull away, he deepened the kiss.

Jordan lost herself in the moment. Or did until a cold nose pressed against her ear. She jerked back at the sensation. "Jenny!"

Michael's eyes flashed open. "What?"

She started to laugh and thumbed at the dog. "Jealous much?"

"Not jealous." Michael groused. "She's probably hungry."

"She's hungry—" Jordan glanced at her watch. "—and I have to get to work."

"Are we good, Madeline?" His forehead wrinkled as he looked down and then back up at her. "This felt right to me. I don't want you to overthink it and shy away."

"We are, Michael." She pressed back to him, showing him exactly how good.

Chapter 10

Jordan's insides began vibrating along with the sound of applause as Olivia made her introduction.

"Ladies and Gentlemen, Jazz House is pleased to welcome Madeline Cielo to the stage."

The CorSam Trio played an Armstrong song. Walking forward, she felt like it was indeed a wonderful world. Ultra-awake, her body fueled with adrenaline, she let Jordan slip away and embodied Madeline. Flashing a broad smile around the room, she grasped offered hands. Moments later, she stood on the small stage.

"Thank you for the amazing welcome," she purred in her chanteuse voice. "And thank you all for joining us. The band—" She waved to Coral, SammyD, and Andre. "—and I would like to take you on a romantic journey tonight with songs of love and hope." She paused, waiting for the applause to die down, and then opened her arms wide. The silver sequins on her flapper-style dress caught and flickered little flashes of light all around. "Come on, climb aboard, and let's fly together."

Like writing a book, the best song sets had a cohesive arc. It took the audience along on a story by song. Her growing feelings for Michael inspired this playlist. It was hard to see past the stage lights, but she knew he was out there.

When the set ended, Jordan made her way back to the dressing room. A soft knock came at the door. While adjusting the silver headband with red and silver feathers, she called, "Give me a second."

A moment later, she cracked the door open and smiled.

"Hi, gorgeous." Michael's grinning face met hers. He slipped into the dressing room.

"Hi, yourself." She wrapped her arms around his neck.

"You were fabulous out there tonight." He murmured into her neck. "I'd love to stay, but duty calls."

In the two weeks since brunch and their first kiss, they'd moved beyond just friends. Except when she and Michael were working, they'd become inseparable. Because of their work and lifestyle, they went on daytime dates. Most often they took walks in the fields and woods near his house with the dogs. Lunch on the weekends. And an occasional matinee before Jordan needed to be at Jazz House.

"I worry about you," she murmured.

"I know you do." He took a loose curl from near her temple and placed it back where it belonged. "Hey, what's this from?"

Her heart dropped into her stomach. "What?"

"This scar."

She flinched when he traced it with his finger. "It's nothing. A childhood fall."

"It doesn't look that old." Michael held her at arm's length. "Must have been a heck of a fall."

Jordan shrugged out of his hands. "Yes, it was."

"Madeline, don't turn away." He reached for her.

"I'm sorry. I didn't mean to pry."

"No." She flashed her stage smile. "You're fine. It was a bad experience, and I don't like to talk about it. Besides, don't you have a job to go to?"

"You knock 'em dead out there." He returned the smile—one that didn't reach his eyes.

"And you be careful out there."

When the door closed after he left, Jordan went to the mirror and brushed the hair away from the scar. Between the stage lights and performance, sweat melted away the cover makeup. It didn't look like a childhood scar. The wound, though fading, was still not flat nor lightening.

Another knock came at the door.

"Who is it?" She retouched the scar with a makeup sponge.

"It's me, Olivia."

"One second." Jordan adjusted her hair to cover her temple, then went to the door.

"I wanted to catch you now in case I'm busy when you're ready to head home." Olivia picked up a red scarf from the chair and folded it. "I saw Michael leave. He's still working the overnight shift?"

Jordan glanced at the clock. She had five more minutes. "Yeah, he's on rotation. After few more shifts, he'll work days for a few weeks. Did you need something in particular? Because I have four minutes to get back on stage, Boss Lady."

Olivia threw the scarf at her.

"Workplace violence?"

"Oh, shut up." Olivia sprawled on the chair. "Shay and I are planning a girls' night. We're going to drink wine and watch movies. I'm sure chocolate and ice cream will be involved."

"I'm in." Jordan stood from the dressing table. "Where and when?"

"Nine tomorrow. David is covering for someone at the hospital. Shay figures she can escape from Aden for one night." Olivia stood, walked to the door, and held it open for Jordan. The band was playing her intro. "My condo. Don't forget to bring your pajamas."

****

Sunday night at Olivia's condo, the women gathered. Jazz House closed early on Sunday and didn't open Mondays, so none of them needed to be up early the next day.

Jordan glanced around at the modern, clean lines of her friend's home. Everything was neat as a pin. The cream-colored sofa with navy pillows sat low and looked comfortable. She loved the color combo. Candles were lit inside the fireplace, and two more flanked an art deco mantel clock. "Nice place, Olivia."

"Thanks." She flipped on the floor lamp. "Help yourself, and don't be shy."

Popcorn, chocolate, wine, and a cheese board enticed from the glass coffee table.

Jordan snagged another piece of cheddar and made a tower with a grape and an olive. She loved the creamy, salty-sweet taste.

"Let's watch a movie." Shay added more wine to Jordan's glass.

"No. No movies. I'll fall asleep." Olivia pulled a deck of cards out of the drawer under the table. "How about a game? We can talk and play."

Jordan leaned forward and picked up the deck. She shuffled it like a pro. Waggling her eyebrows up and down, she said, "What's your game, ladies? Poker? Blackjack?"

"Oh, no." Olivia took the deck from her. "No card sharks allowed."

"How about Go Fish?" Jordan teased her with an eye roll.

"How about Kings in the Corner?" Olivia tossed a popcorn kernel at her.

"Never played that." Shay pulled pj's out of the duffel bag. There were cat images all over them.

Laughter burst out of Jordan. "Those are hysterical. Do you wear them around Aden?"

Shay blushed, turned on her heel, and stalked to the doorway for the bathroom. Over her shoulder, she said with a toss of her head, "That is none of your business."

Both Jordan and Olivia squealed with glee.

"I'm glad you joined us tonight." Olivia handed her the glass of wine.

"I am too."

Another bout of laughter erupted when Shay returned wearing the silly pajamas. She stuck her tongue out at them. "What's this game?"

"Kings in the Corner." Olivia plopped down onto one of the big floor pillows. "It's easy."

"I used to play it with my grandma." Jordan took the cards back. "You know how to play solitaire, right."

Silence. She glanced up. "What are you both staring at?"

Olivia plucked at a pillow tassel. "Nothing, really. You've just never mentioned family."

Jordan raised an eyebrow. "Well, I had one."

"Yeah, but…"

"No personal history." Shay sat on the ottoman.

"That was your rule."

"Geez, guys." Jordan gazed at the two women. "It's not a deep dark secret to have a grandma."

"Okay, cheers to grandmas."

They lifted their glasses.

"To Grandma Grace." Shay took a sip.

Olivia smiled. "To Grandmas Elise and Rose."

Her heart beat faster. "To Grandma Jordan."

It was the first time she'd said her real name out loud. Tears threatened, but she took a drink of wine and set the glass down. "Let's play."

A few rounds of cards and wine later, Shay burped. "I can't play anymore. Since history is out, how about the present?"

The other women looked at her.

Suspicion aroused, Jordan eyed them both. "Did you think a few glasses of wine would make me loose-lipped about Michael?"

"Well, yes." Olivia blinked like an owl.

Jordan heaved herself off the floor and walked over to the sideboard where frames held pictures. Family. How she missed hers. "Who's this?"

"That would be the previously toasted Grandma Elise holding hands with Aden and me. We were about four." Olivia came and stood beside her. "Here's my mom and dad." She pointed at a smiling couple. A blonde woman who resembled Olivia was under the tall, dark-haired man's arm."

Jordan took the picture and studied it. "They look happy."

"They were, for the most part." Olivia traced the picture of her father. "Dad died in a car accident. A few years later, my mom and I were discussing relationships. She told me that for a short time, they'd separated. Then when they found out she was pregnant, he came home."

"I guess all families have their drama." Jordan placed the picture back gently. God, she missed her own family so much. She walked over to the coffee table and lifted her glass. After taking a sip, she plopped onto the sofa. "The reason I don't talk about my family is to keep them safe."

She clapped a hand over her mouth. *In vino veritas.* The wine did loosen her lips.

Shay leaned forward from her place on the floor. "What do you mean, Madeline?"

Jordan bowed her head, closed her eyes, and bit her tongue. The cushion next to her sank. A warm hand covered hers, which she'd folded on her lap. When she peeked up, Olivia's compassionate brown eyes peered into hers.

Oh, she wanted to tell. *No!* There was no way she would endanger these women. Instead, she plastered on her stage smile. "Don't mind me. It's a long story, and I don't want to talk about it. Just deal the cards."

Shay and Olivia shared a look between them.

Cheese and rice, this wasn't over. She took another swallow of wine.

****

Business, world-news, crime, one never knew where opportunities would pop up. And they always did.

Since the time he could read, his father would instruct on the signs to look for.

Greed in the world was rampant. Countries vied for supremacy. Often, if you were intelligent and alert, even slight interference with money or politics could make tides turn and fill his bank accounts with cash.

For years he'd closely watched Grigory Sokolov and what the man had accomplished in the eastern countries. Now that Grigory was gone, the places he'd interfered in were still at, or on the brink of, war. Over the last few months, Kyrios invested heavily to keep them unstable.

There was a knock at the door. He growled at the interruption. "Who is it?"

"Tito."

"Come in." Kyrios looked up from one of the Greek newspapers he scoured each day.

The heavily muscled man entered the room and pulled off his dark sunglasses, revealing the still-livid scar from the nightclub fire. "We may have a lead."

"What kind of lead?"

"Your wife."

Kyrios cheek twitched. Tito didn't need to know he'd had the marriage annulled the moment he discovered Jordan hadn't died but rather ran from him. If anything happened to him, he refused to leave her a merry and rich widow.

"She made it back to the United States with a false passport." Tito crossed the room, tucking the dark glasses into his jacket pocket. "One of my men found the man who forged her papers. Airport records show she flew into JFK early December."

Kyrios set the newspaper down, went to the bar, poured a tsipouro shot, and tossed it back—the harsh bitterness welcome. He made Tito wait while he popped an olive into his mouth, chewed, and then poured a second drink.

"Ahh, my lovely Jordan." He carried the tsipouro over to the white leather club chair and sat, placing the glass on a side table. "She could be anywhere."

The man pulled a magazine from his inside jacket pocket and handed it to Kyrios. *Slate Quarry News*. He lifted an eyebrow at Tito.

"Page six."

Kyrios riffled through to an article titled *Sumptuous Food and Swinging Jazz come to the Poconos*. Mark Ellis, a food journalist from the local paper, detailed a story about Jazz House. Near the end of the article, it said for more pictures, turn to page eleven.

At first, he didn't see it, but he rescanned the photo. There she was. In a group shot near the corner of the bar—likely unaware the camera had used a panoramic view. And there—another picture. One in silhouette. But he'd recognize his woman anywhere.

"Do we have an advance team in the States?"

"Yes." Tito nodded. "Anatole and his American cousin Luka are preparing for your visit to Philadelphia."

"Send them up to this"—he scanned the magazine—"Jazz House and scout the area."

"Yes, Kyrie."

"And make arrangements to move our trip up." The business trip suddenly became more exciting. He was on the hunt now.

"I also hired a new investigator to search in the States," Tito said in Greek. "He is discreet and thorough. A former cop with no loyalty to the organization."

"A cop?" Kyrios glared at Tito. "Are you sure he's

not a plant?"

Tito snorted. "Absolutely. He turned against his people."

"Why?"

"What else?" The big man shrugged. "A woman."

This time Kyrios snorted. What else, indeed.

When Tito left, Kyrios stood and walked to the open glass door. He stepped out onto the patio. The Mediterranean sparkled. A cool breeze ruffled his hair. He lit a cigar and puffed. The tobacco overwhelmed the scent of a nearby hyacinth. He smiled around the Cuban's brown leaf.

Chapter 11

The creaking of saddle leather and the jingle of bridles kept time to the thudding of hooves on the trail.

The birds flitted and twittered through the still-naked branches.

Nature's music filled Jordan, and happiness bubbled in her chest. "I'd like to come back here when the leaves are out."

Michael reined his horse, Jack, up next to her. "Something for us to look forward to."

"I remember my grandpa's barn. The smell of horses." She patted Rose's neck. "He taught me to ride when I was a young girl."

"Your grandpa?" Michael blinked, opened his mouth, then shut it.

Her heart ached at his pained expression. "Like I told Olivia, I had a family."

He scratched his forehead. "I just don't know what's taboo and what we can talk about."

"I'm sorry." Jordan sighed and pulled the mare to a halt. Bands of regret tightened around her chest. "I've made this so hard for you."

When he turned his gelding around, the pinched look on his face seared her heart before he turned his head.

"It's fine. I signed up for this."

"No." She urged her horse closer. Leaning over,

she laid a hand on his arm. "You didn't sign up for worry and frustration."

He covered her hand. "I promised."

"Let's do this." She tilted her head and considered her words. "We talk like normal people. If something heads into what I think of as off-limits...I'll...kiss you instead."

The smile that erupted on his face melted her heart. The mischievous twinkle with a crinkle at the corner of his gingerbread-brown eyes made her insides turn gooey.

"Madeline, where are you from?"

She slid her hand up his biceps, then pulled his aviators off and tucked them into the neck of his shirt. "Silly man."

Whether he leaned in, or she pulled him closer didn't matter. Warm, full lips pressed against hers. How could lips be soft and firm at the same time? She sighed.

Jordan tipped her head farther when Michael deepened the kiss. He tasted like the cherry fruit rings he always carried. Breathless moments later, he pulled away, but not before leaving small, gentle kisses to ease the separation.

"Woman, you have the best ideas." He pressed his forehead to hers. Jack stomped a hoof with impatience, and Michael pulled back and dismounted. "Come on. Let's walk for a while."

He grasped the mare's reins while she climbed down on legs so wobbly, it was amazing she didn't fall. "I could use a break. My legs and definitely my bum need one."

She gathered Rose's reins from him, and they

walked along the rails-to-trails path. At first, her muscles complained, but soon they loosened up. "I forgot how much I enjoy being outdoors and in nature."

Though it was barely spring, some of the early bloomers stuck their intrepid faces out from the loam. Rare trumpets of white trillium and yellow coltsfoot gave the mostly drab woods some color.

Jordan took a deep breath. Fallen leaves and needles from pine trees mixed and lay on the ground, adding a musty, earthy smell. It wasn't entirely pleasant nor offensive. Just the earth renewing itself. "Did you hear that? Was that an owl?"

Michael took her free hand in his big warm one. "No. I think it was mourning doves. They're often mistaken for each other."

A flash of reddish orange caught her attention. "Oh, look! A robin. Spring is on its way."

"You would never know, after seeing you all fancy at the club, that at heart, you're a country girl."

"I am. For a long time, I was stifled and closed in." She gasped and slipped her hand out of his. Walking away from him, she tugged her sleeves. *Stupid. Watch what you say.*

"What do you mean *closed in*?"

With a wave of her hand, she answered, "You know how city life can be. Exciting and fun but also oppressive at times. All the stone and concrete. It's good to get out of town and into nature."

"That's not what you meant." Michael followed and placed his hand on her shoulder. "Sweetheart? Do you still not trust me?"

Jordan turned to him, intending to kiss him to end the questioning, but instead blurted out, "I want to tell you something." A gasped sob worked its way out of her chest. "But I'm scared of the possible ramifications."

He cocked his head. "Madeline, it's okay. I'm safe."

"Each time I left the house when I was young, my mother used to tell me, *Make good choices.*" Tears welled in her eyes, but she refused to let them fall. "I made a bad choice."

"Come with me." He took Rose's reins and led the two horses over to the side of the trail, where the sun shone down in a small open space onto a boulder.

When he lifted Jordan onto the warm surface, she pulled her knees up and hugged them to her chest.

Birds twittered in the woods, and the horses munching on the bonus patch of green from the protected area were loud against her silence.

Michael leaned next to the rock beside her and pulled off his sunglasses. "I think we've all made some bad choices."

She snorted. "How about horrendous choices?"

"You told me you weren't a criminal." His tone dropped low. "What could be so terrible?"

The boulder was big enough to lay back on, so she did. With her arm over her face and eyes screwed shut, she wondered if her heart would beat its way out of her chest. Could she open up to him? *Dear God, I need someone to talk to. I know you listen, but two-way conversations are pretty helpful sometimes. Please let Michael understand, and will you keep us safe if I do?*

Make good choices, granddaughter. She took a deep breath and sat back up.

"I was married to a very bad man." Her voice

shook. "You're right. I told you the law didn't want me." She leaned her head back and looked up at the sky, blinking back tears. "But I'm wanted by a man who I'm pretty sure *is* a criminal."

****

What would he do if she were a criminal? Could he let her go? *No* came the resounding thought. *No way.*

"Who?" Michael urged her to go on. "And what do you mean, you're pretty sure *he* is?"

She turned to face him. "My real name is Jordan.

"And?" Michael's stomach flipped. Could he deal with the truth? *Yes, man. You love her.*

"Vasilakis. His name is Kyrios Vasilakis."

"The Greek billionaire?" Michael blanched, and buzzing started in his ears.

She bit her lower lip and nodded. "Did you hear about the burning of a nightclub called Lunae Lucem in Greece a while back?"

"Yeah. It was all over the news." His Adam's apple bobbed. "They reported his wife died in the fire."

"No, Michael." She lay down again and curled up on the rock's hard surface. "She escaped."

He climbed up and curled around her, trying to offer comfort. "Tell me."

Once she started, words poured out like an infection from a wound. She told him of years of abuse, isolation, and threats, then finished with, "He hurt me. Emotionally, physically, and spiritually."

Each word was a punch to Michael's gut. He held the trembling woman in his arms though all he wanted to do was find something to kick and punch. But this wasn't about him, so he lay still except for stroking her hair until the bubble of warmth grew cold and uncomfortable. "Let's go home."

She nodded.

Once she was steady on her feet, he gathered the horses. She felt so fragile when he helped her into Rose's saddle.

Even the horses seemed to sense their moods, and there was no trying to snatch bites of grass or leaves as they headed back to the truck.

As soon as the vehicle came into sight, he pushed the auto-start button to warm it up. He tucked her into the front seat while he trailered the horses.

The ride back to Michael's house screamed with silence. After putting the dogs in the yard, he led her into the house, wrapped her shivering frame in a blanket, and then lit a fire. "I have to go settle the horses."

"Do what you have to do." She nodded and stared into the flames. "I'll be fine."

Rose and Jack entered the stalls without any coaxing.

While he tossed a few flakes of hay into the rack, Jack nudged him. He stroked the long white blaze. "People can suck, my friend."

A soft nicker, which he assumed was an agreement, answered.

While the two munched their food, he gathered up the dogs and returned to the house, going directly to the kitchen. While the kettle heated, he stared out into the yard, running a hand over his head. How could he fix this? Or should he extract himself and let the authorities take over? *No.* Madeline—wait—Jordan was part of him now. She was as much his heart as the arteries and muscles. The kettle whistled, and he filled the cups.

Soon the scent of spiced chai filled the kitchen. It was a good strong tea to warm someone to their toes.

Michael carried the cups to the living room, noting Jordan hadn't stirred. He carefully sat next to her on the sofa.

Even the dogs didn't crowd for attention.

"Tell me about the night you got away." He gently prodded while pressing the hot mug into her hands.

Icy fingers wrapped around it. She inhaled deeply, not looking at him.

"I want to know everything." He needed her to trust him. "Sweetheart, believe in me, as I believe in you."

She sipped the blend of black tea that scented the air with ginger, cloves, cardamom, and cinnamon. After setting the cup carefully on the coaster, she pulled the blanket tighter around her bowed shoulders.

"There was a man on the balcony above the dining room. He wore black clothing." Her voice remained flat, like she was speaking of someone else. "He was like you see on television. What mercenaries wear."

Michael's hands hurt from gripping the teacup. He couldn't put it down, needing something to ground him as he listened. "It wasn't an accidental fire like the news reported?"

"No." She stared into the fireplace. "I think a bomb of some kind went off that night. Maybe more than one."

Michael's cup clunked when he set it on the coffee table, then he hitched his leg underneath to face her. The hair on the back of his neck stood on end. If Madeline—*no, Jordan*—wasn't as strong as she was, she could've died before he ever met her. "You are amazing. Brave. I'm here. I promise we'll find a way out of this.

****

Despite the fire snapping and crackling, she thought she'd never be warm again. A shiver ran through her body, and she nearly spilled the tea.

Michael took the cup from her and then grabbed the cabin-themed quilt with pine trees and bears from a nearby chair and laid it over her shoulders as well. "Take your time. Know you're safe here with me."

She nodded and clutched at the quilt, cocooning it around her body. "At first, I didn't know what was happening. People started screaming. Shots rang out. The men wearing black swarmed the room. I ran off stage and out through the kitchen."

"You got away safely when others didn't. That's a miracle." Michael leaned with his forearms on his thighs.

"I got away." She flinched when a log settled in the fire, then reached for a tissue from the end table. "Not safely.

She lifted the hair from the side of her temple and wiped the covering makeup away.

Michael's gaze darted to her hairline where he'd noticed her scar.

"The scar you saw? It's from a bullet graze."

"You nearly died." Michael leaped to his feet and began to pace, his hands running through his hair, making a mess of it. "There were so many times you could have been killed."

She never knew such a group of pacers. Aden, Olivia, and now Michael all trod a path on the floor when agitated.

"I nearly passed out but knew I could die in the fire—or worse, Kyrios would find me." Jordan squinched her eyes shut. "I forced myself to push through it. I made my way to the kitchen, and the back door was open." Her leg began to bob. "I'd reached it and was nearly through, and that's when the explosion happened."

Michael squatted next to her, reached into the blanket, and grasped her hands. His were so warm against the chill of hers. "You don't have to go on right now."

"No." She inhaled a sharp breath and straightened her spine. "If I don't do this now, I may never."

He sat back on the couch, pulled her over, and tucked her under his arm. "Okay, let's get it all out in the air and then figure out a way forward."

Jordan nodded and curled into his side. "The blast thrust me outside the door. I landed on my hands and knees. At first, I couldn't hear anything. There was a tree nearby. I crawled to it and hid on the opposite side."

Michael's heart pounded in her ear. "My God. You probably had a concussion."

Nodding, she snaked her hand out of the blanket and covered his heart. "Probably, but the explosion gave me the chance I needed. My hearing slowly returned, and I could make out sirens getting louder. Flashing blue-and-red lights made everything surreal."

Arms tightened around her.

Jenny whined, rose from her place by the fire, and laid her muzzle on Jordan's legs.

"It's okay, girl." Jordan ran her hand over the black-and-tan head with its sorrowful eyes. "I'm all right now."

"Where did you go?" Michael's voice was tight and low. "Who helped you?"

"No one." Jordan swallowed hard. "I made my way back to the house."

Michael jumped up and strode over to the sliding glass door. "What do you mean, you went back to the house?"

Jordan jerked back. "I had to. I needed money, clothes. How far would a woman covered in blood get before someone stopped her?"

Hands tunneled through his hair. "I'm sorry. I didn't mean to bellow like that. You're right. Even with a possible concussion, you were thinking. Please, forgive me?"

Jordan bit her bottom lip and nodded. "It's okay."

"It's not okay." He slowly returned to the couch but sat instead on the coffee table in front of her and held out his hand. When she reached out and took it, he let out a sigh. "Tell me the rest?"

"Not much to tell." Taking back her hand, she stood and walked over to the fireplace. She squatted and held her palms out toward the warmth.

"Kyrios made me dress the way he liked, but I'd kept my old clothes hidden away in a suitcase in the back of the closet. He is careless about leaving money around." She shrugged. "He never missed it when I pinched some here and there, stashing it until the day I needed it."

Michael went over, lowered himself down onto the braided rug by the hearth, and sat cross-legged. "This all happened a year ago. What did you do during that time? How did you live?"

"At heart, I'm a country girl. A country girl can survive." A smile ghosted across her face as she almost quoted the Williams song. "I slept rough sometimes. Worked here and there for a few dollars. Squirreled it away." She shrugged. "Sang for my supper, as it were. You'd be amazed at how much a person can sometimes make busking on street corners and in parks. I worked my way across Europe. Most of the money went for a false ID and passport."

"And you ended up in Northeast Pennsylvania," Michael whispered. "I'm glad you did."

Now they both sat facing each other cross-legged in front of the fire.

"You can't tell anyone." Her voice came out a harsh whisper. "The only thing keeping not only me, but my family safe, is that Jordan Vasilakis died in a terrible incident."

"Your family believes you're dead?"

She stared down at her hands. "It's the only way."

"We have to do something." His words were low pitched and determined. "I'll help you. Together we can fix this."

"No, Michael." Her chin quivered. "You promised. Don't make me run again."

"Come here." He pulled her to him, and they spooned in silence, staring into the fire.

Chapter 12

Michael lifted his head and stared out the window. He rubbed his eyes with the heels of his hands. Since taking Madeline—*no, Jordan*—home yesterday, he'd spent countless hours in front of the computer screen.

When his vision cleared, he noticed the mess on his usually neat dining room table. Empty coffee cups and paper plates with half-eaten sandwiches were strewn about. Sometime near dawn, he'd fallen asleep, and now his neck ached all the way into his shoulder.

He reached up, crossed an arm over his chest, and dug his fingers into the knot while rolling his head. One of his vertebrae cracked.

Woof.

Jenny sat by the back door, giving him the stink-eye.

There were several more cracks in his spine when he stood to let her out. Forest came out of nowhere, nearly plowing him over. "Sorry, guys."

The air was cold. The sun still hadn't breached the tree line. He took a deep breath, and his head cleared. Love for him was never a straight road.

While the dogs patrolled the yard, Michael filled their dishes with food and fresh water, then opened the fridge. As he scrambled eggs, he ruminated about what he'd learned. Not much.

There'd been a lot of speculation about Kyrios

Vasilakis over the years. Accusations of trading in weapons and drugs were rampant. Charges of money laundering and financing terrorists never stuck. The man even eluded several murder charges.

The eggs sizzled in the pan, and Michael stirred them around, then pushed down the toaster button. When everything was finished, he sat back at the table eating while watching the dogs running the fence line in the early dawn. The two horses grazed in the field behind them—a peaceful scene. Dear God, when did his life get so complicated?

He cared about Madeline—*no*—Jordan. But she'd made him promise not to say or do anything. He was a cop, dammit. How could he stand by and do nothing while she lived a life of fear? Not to mention, allowing a criminal to get away with whatever unscrupulous behavior he dabbled in?

What was his responsibility here? What about culpability? Jordan was on the run, living under an alias. Was there a legality here that, if not broken, was bending?

He stood and cleaned up the mess, loading the plates into the dishwasher. Next up, a shower.

"Swwwttttt!" He whistled at the door.

The dogs skittered across the tile and buried their faces in their dishes. He rolled his eyes. Every meal was like their last.

While the water heated, he texted Sergeant Romano.

—Do you have time for a sit-down today?—

Then he added:

—Unofficially —

He'd keep Jordan's name out of it. But sometimes

a person needed guidance, especially in such a serious situation. He trusted Alyssa to be discreet.

His phone vibrated.

—Coffee before your shift and after mine.—

—Sounds good.—

He was on second shift today. It would give him time to stop by the St. Francis shelter with the bags of cat and dog food he'd collected at the police station. St. Francis did its part in helping the homeless population in town. Often people would rather sleep in their car or on the street than give up a beloved pet. The church had opened a shelter that welcomed both. They also provided veterinary services, including neutering and vaccinations.

By the time his errands were done, Jordan should be awake.

****

Jordan sat at the small white bistro table, sipping a hot mocha and staring out the window at the rooftop across the street. Not much of a view, but past that, farther out, the Pocono Mountains rose. The tops still had snow.

After tossing and turning most of the night, she finally gave up on sleep around three. "Lord, what did I do?"

In a moment of weakness, she'd told Michael everything. She was glad of his comfort, but last night, when he drove her home, there was a stilted silence between them. He'd walked her to the door, kissed her forehead gently, then turned and walked away. Was it a goodbye kiss?

It was still early. The sun, trying to peek through the clouds, painted yellow, pink, and orange swaths on the horizon.

She picked up her phone. Six-thirty. No calls, no texts. Michael was probably still sleeping. She pulled the rainbow-colored afghan blanket tighter around her shoulders.

"Ugh." Her coffee was cold now. Cold, like her hands. Cold, like her heart. "Stop wallowing."

Jordan pushed away from the table and started straightening up. The paperback romance with the cop on the front caught her attention. The dark-haired model on the cover resembled Michael. Her breath hitched. An old song came to mind. *What will be will be.* She began to hum it. Too bad she didn't have a crystal ball.

A little while later, the apartment spotless, she got dressed. Having no agenda for the day left her feeling rudderless. Maybe she'd head over to the library again. Her phone vibrated on the kitchen table.

—Are you awake?—

Michael. Her chest tightened.

—Yes. —

—Can I come over?—

She stared at the phone. Darn text messages. They gave no hint as to the emotion behind the words. Did he miss her? Had he decided to end the growing relationship? With a shake of her head, she tapped out.

—I'll put a pot of coffee on.—

—See you in a few.—

Her stomach churned. Coffee wasn't going to be her friend. Instead, she put on a kettle of water and took out an old French press she'd discovered in a box of thrift-store kitchen appliances. A canister with herbal tea was next to it, and she chose a bag of lemon balm.

No matter what happened between them, she needed the anti-anxiety herb.

A short while later, the doorbell rang, and she glanced at the security camera. The grainy image made her heart catch. She buzzed Michael in. Moments later, his large frame filled her doorway, and their eyes met. Jordan swallowed hard.

His lips, pressed together, made a thin line, and drawn eyebrows carved a vee on his forehead.

"Hi," she said.

Michael's face softened, and he ran his thumb down her cheek. "Hi."

She stepped back. "Come on in."

He walked past, stopped in the middle of the studio, and looked around. It was the first time he'd been in her apartment.

She tried to see the room through his eyes. It was a little shabby. Certainly not like his cabin. The kettle startled her out of the depressing thoughts, and she scurried past the room divider into the kitchenette. "I changed mine to tea, but I'll pour your coffee."

She started to fill the press with shaky hands when a large masculine one covered and steadied hers. Her shoulders slumped. "I'm sorry I involved you. It's okay if you don't want to get caught up in the mess that's my life."

"What are you talking about?" His words blew a puff of air into her ear.

"Well, you didn't say much last night driving me home. And obviously, the look on your face now isn't a happy one." Jordan choked up. "I understand. It's a lot of baggage."

He guided her hand to set the kettle down then

turned her around.

She leaned her forehead into his chest, unable to look him in the eye. He wrapped his arms around her and held her in a comforting embrace.

Michael rested his head on top of hers. "I'll admit, it seemed overwhelming at first. I guess that's why I was so quiet. But I'm not going anywhere."

She sagged against him when her legs became weak. "I'm happy and terrified at the same time."

"Why terrified?"

"Because if anything happens to you, I don't know what I'll do."

"Look." He led her over to the small sofa and pulled her onto his lap. "We do need to talk about it."

"I don't want to," she mumbled. "If I never see Kyrios or hear his name again, it'll be the best thing."

"I know, sweetheart." He lifted her chin and gazed into her eyes. "But being aware of what he's up to is important."

Jordan pulled away and scooted to the other end of the sofa. She tucked her knees and drew the pillow to her chest. "Okay."

"You know he's planning on coming to the States, right?"

"Yes, I found out the morning we had coffee for the first time." She looked past him to the window. "You asked me what was wrong, and I said nothing. I lied. Everything was wrong."

"Do you have any indication that he may be coming for you?"

She gave him a small tight shake of the head. "Not really. Kyrios goes on many business trips. This seems like a normal one. Besides, I've been very careful."

"I want you to think about something."

"No."

"Look at me." He laid a hand on her knee.

"No, I can't do it." She closed her eyes and shook her head. "Please don't ask me to."

"How do you plan to live the rest of your life?"

His voice was soft, but the words hit her like a giant gong reverberating through her nerves. She shook her head more vehemently. "I won't go to the authorities. It will be like ringing a dinner bell if we tell anyone, a dinner bell that says, *here she is, Kyrios. Come and get her.*"

"My sergeant is very discreet."

Jordan covered her face with both hands and sank deeper into the cushion. "You're right. I know you're right." She pulled her hands away and hugged the pillow tighter. "But, Michael, I'm so scared."

She tossed the pillow to the floor and moved back over to Michael's lap.

He wrapped both arms around her as she lay her head in the crook of his shoulder and rocked her gently. "I've got you," he murmured. "I won't let anything happen to you."

A short while later, she got up to carry their cups to the kitchenette sink. When she returned, her cheeks warmed. He'd picked up the paperback off the table.

"Cop romance?"

"Yeah." She grabbed it and held it behind her back. "Girl's gotta dream."

"Harrumph." He kicked back with his hand hooked behind his head with a smug face. "Thought I had that covered."

She first threw the book at him and then launched

herself, landing back in his lap.

****

"Come in."

Michael opened the door to Sgt. Romano's office and stepped into the polar opposite of Lt. Morgan's.

Diplomas, certifications, and commendations lined the walls alongside pictures of family and family vacations.

Michael often envied the close family ties she maintained even with her demanding job. One time he'd been invited to a birthday picnic at Slate Quarry Park, organized by her paramedic husband, Matteo. Michael had been uncomfortable at first. He had a hard enough time keeping up with her brothers and sisters. There were cousins, second cousins, and cousins with no blood connection at all. Kids ran everywhere. He wasn't used to all the hugging and loud, boisterous conversations.

The woman who sat across the desk from him now had spotted Michael standing alone off to the side. A few minutes later, she'd introduced him around as their newest cousin, and the family enfolded him into their clan. To this day, he received cards and invitations to weddings and baptisms.

"Hey, cuz. Come on in and shut the door." Alyssa tapped the keys on the laptop. "Give me a minute. This scheduling is giving me fits."

He perused the pictures on the wall. There were several new babies, and he did a double take when he spied himself and his *cousins* at the party. "I made the wall?"

"Yeah, you did." Sarge closed the computer. "Now, how can I help you?"

Pausing, he took a seat in the cracked brown vinyl chair across from her and fiddled with his hat.

An eyebrow lifted, and she sat back in her chair. "That bad?"

Michael cleared his throat. "It has the potential to be."

They stared at each other for a moment before she said, "Break it down."

"Have you ever heard of Kyrios Vasilakis?"

"Machau, what have you gotten yourself into?" Piercing dark eyes nearly scorched him as she glared across the desk. Cousin Alyssa disappeared, and Sgt. Romano took over.

Michael cleared his throat once more, then started at the beginning. An hour later, he finished with, "Jordan is in my life. We need to figure out how to protect and extract her from this situation."

A huge puff of air escaped her pursed lips, and she scratched the side of her head and cursed. "No trouble out of you for years. Now it's a runaway train coming into the home station."

He shrugged, running both hands through his hair. "Sorry."

"Give me a couple of days." She stood, walked to the window, and looked out. "I know some people. It's their job to be discreet."

"Thanks, Sarge." He stood and went to the door.

"Michael?"

He paused with his hand on the knob and turned his head. "Yeah?"

"I'm glad you found someone."

Rubbing the back of his neck, he said, "Me, too."

Chapter 13

Jordan paused, staring at her reflection in the smokey glass door to Jazz House. The woman looking back at her appeared happy and confident. It mirrored how she felt inside. Sharing her story with Michael was like popping a blister. The pain eased, knowing she wasn't alone in this any longer.

For the past few days, the weight she'd carried even before the night of the fire lifted, and it was like she walked on air.

Michael kept his word. He agreed to keep calling her Madeline even when they were alone. They didn't want to take a chance on slipping up. He didn't push her about family or where they were. There was no way she'd endanger Momma and Grandma.

He'd spoken with his sergeant, Alyssa Romano, and she'd told him she'd discreetly look into the situation, and she was friends with some federal agents.

Jordan made her way through Jazz House. The smell of the southern holy trinity—onions, celery, and bell peppers—tickled her nose. The yeasty scent of bread baking backed these up. Her tummy rumbled.

"Olivia, come on. Don't let one pompous blogger steal your happiness." The voices came from the direction of the office.

They were at it again, arguing like sisters.

Jordan shook her head.

"Ticktock, Shay. Our chat is over. Besides, I think I smell something burning in the kitchen."

"We're not done talking." Shay lifted her chin and marched past Jordan. She called out over her shoulder, "And food does not burn in my kitchen."

Jordan laughed until Olivia walked from the office hallway into the dining room. "Are you all right?"

Dark circles under Olivia's eyes stood out against her pale skin. "I'm fine. Why does everyone keep asking me?"

"You just..." Jordan trailed off. Olivia never pried into her personal life. The least Jordan could do was respect her privacy. "Never mind."

"I'm sorry. I didn't mean to bark at you." Olivia sat on the edge of the stage and put her head in her hands. "I have a headache is all."

Jordan sat next to her and placed an arm around the woman's shoulders. "I read the blog too. Try not to worry, Olivia. It's only one guy."

"But an important one." The frazzled woman leaned into her. "A lot of people read his blog. Not to mention Michael told Aden the guy might be in cahoots with Kayla."

"The jerk's probably a misogynist who believes the only kitchen a woman should be in is the one at home." Jordan gave her a hug. "You and I both know Jazz House is fabulous. And as far as this Kayla is concerned, she's disappeared, hasn't she? No one has seen anything of her?"

"No." Olivia peeked up through her fingers and then sat up. "And yes, we are fabulous. You helped make us that. I don't want to lose you."

"I'm not planning on going anywhere." Jordan's

circle of people had certainly grown. A twinge of pain squeezed her heart at the thought of leaving. "I don't make friends easily."

"Me either. But maybe we can practice with each other." Olivia pulled herself straight, tossed her hair back, and extended her hand. "Madeline, will you be my friend?"

Jordan grasped Olivia's hand. "I would love to be your friend."

"I want to be friends too."

They both spun to face the kitchen where Shay stood in the doorway, pouting.

"Shay, you can't be my friend. You're my sister." Olivia lifted her hands in mock exasperation.

Jordan patted the stage next to where she sat. "Come on. There's room here. I'll be your friend."

Shay perched next to her and enveloped Jordan in a hug. "Thank you for not being mean like Olivia."

The three burst out in hysterics. It was good to laugh. How long had it been since she'd experienced the grab your sides and howl until your ribs hurt? Too long.

****

Raucous hilarity drew Michael into Jazz House after he parked the car. He leaned against the doorjamb regarding the three women he'd grown so fond of, who were giggling and carrying on like teenagers.

When they composed themselves, Jordan noticed him first. Their gazes locked over the distance.

Olivia was next. She leaned over and whispered something to Shay, and the two of them started snickering again.

Jordan gave both of them a pinch without breaking

eye contact. "Cut it out. I can unfriend you."

"Let's go, Shay." Olivia hauled the other woman to her feet. "Let them have privacy."

Arm in arm, the two tittered their way to the kitchen.

"Hi."

"Hi." He skirted smoothly around the tables between them. "I wanted to see you before you started working."

"I'm glad." Jordan stood and smoothed out her shirt. "How long were you standing there?"

He shook his head. "Not long." He snaked his arm around her waist and pulled her close, savoring the scents of vanilla and jasmine drifting lightly around her. He wrapped the other arm around her and buried his nose in her neck. "You always smell so good."

When her head tilted to give more access, he kissed her from shoulder to ear, causing a tremor to run through her body.

The hands curled against his chest opened, and she pushed him away gently. "I'll call in sick."

"I think your girls will know you're lying."

Jordan took his face between her hands and kissed him. "Yeah, they would."

"But I'm off tonight. Do you mind if I stay and listen to your sets?" Michael nuzzled her nose with his. "We could go to the diner afterward. Then I could drop you home." Before she could answer, his phone dinged and vibrated. "Sorry, it's work. I need to take the call."

"It's fine. I have to get ready anyway." She kissed his cheek. "See you in a bit." She sauntered into the back hallway.

His gaze followed until she disappeared into the

dressing room. "Machau," he said into the phone.

"I need you to come in." Sergeant Romano spoke in a hoarse monotone.

"Why? What's up?"

"I had three call-outs." She sniffled. "The flu is running through the department."

"You don't sound good yourself." He sighed. So much for plans with Jordan. "Give me an hour."

"You're good people, Machau." Romano coughed on the other end. "I have a feeling it's going to be a long night."

"Great." He ended the call.

"You're still here?" Olivia was back. "Keep bothering my talent, and I'll summon the cops."

"Go ahead. I'll be the one responding." He waved the phone at her. "I just got called in to work."

"I'm sorry." She set down the vase of red carnations in her hands. "Want a coffee to go?"

"That'd be great." He walked past her toward the back. "I have to let Madeline know I can't stay." He rapped a knuckle on the door three times.

"Just a minute." Rustling sounds. Then the door cracked open. "Hey, impatient man." A big smile appeared on her face, and she opened the door farther. "Come on in. I'm putting my face on."

Leaning against the doorframe, he ran a hand through his hair. "I can't stay."

She glanced up, looking at him through the mirror's reflection. "Is everything okay?"

"Yeah. Well, no." His gaze held hers as he closed the distance between them, and his arms wrapped around her from behind. "The call was from work. They need me to go in."

She leaned back against him. "Is something wrong?"

"The flu is making its way through the department." He nuzzled her neck.

"I understand." She turned in his arms and then stepped back. "We both have responsibilities…"

Narrowing his eyes, he growled and reached for her. "I don't want to go."

"…which require adulting," she finished with a laugh. "Besides, I don't want you to get tired of me."

"Not going to happen."

"Go on. Get out of here." She stood straight and tossed her head in the imitation of a diva. "I have a show to do."

"All right. I'm going, prima donna." He winked from the doorway. "I'll talk to you tomorrow."

"Be careful out there, officer." She blew him a kiss.

"Yes, ma'am." Returning it with a jaunty salute, he promised to be careful.

He popped on his aviator sunglasses and climbed into the truck. While driving to the station, he mulled over the Kyrios situation. Maybe he'd find some downtime and use the department computers to do more research. There was no way he'd let her live the rest of her life in fear and danger. Not if he had anything to say about it.

A few hours later, frustration sizzled in Michael. His jaw ached from clenching it while he cuffed the belligerent drunk. He refrained from shoving the guy into the car and instead protected the man's head as he fell into the back seat.

"Do not…" He pointed a finger at him. "I repeat,

do not throw up in my car."

"I'm cool, man." The drunk lurched sideways. "I'm cool."

Michael slammed the door. He could've been enjoying a night of listening to his woman sing. But no, instead, he was running from one moronic dispatch to another.

"Hey, Officer Machau, rough night?" Shay walked over to him, the stripes from her EMT uniform reflecting the lights from passing vehicles. "My patient refused treatment. Is your guy okay?"

"He's good." He smiled down at the woman he once thought he loved. Well, he did sort of love her, but in a sister-brother way. "How are you and that guy who stole you from me doing?"

Red blossomed in her cheeks.

"That good, huh."

"Stop teasing me." She punched him in the arm.

"Hey, you want to end up in jail for assaulting a police officer?" He rubbed his arm. The woman was strong.

"I'll be your witness." Joanna, her partner, called over from the ambulance. "Especially if she doesn't get over here and help."

Michael shook his head at the partners' antics. Even in the craziest of circumstances, they remained cool, calm, and most often comical. Volunteers were a different breed. All first responders, including police, were. But the volunteers did it for nothing. Put themselves in danger and gave up their free time to help others.

Thinking of free time, he glanced at his watch. Only four more hours until the end of his shift. He'd get a few hours' sleep and then call Jordan. Hopefully, she didn't get all up in her head and start worrying again. Maybe they could grab lunch.

"Hey, I have to go to the bathroom." The drunk pounded on the window. "I wanna go home."

"Shut up." Michael banged back. "You're going someplace, but it's not home."

With a final glance to make sure the traffic was clear, he stepped around the patrol car. Out of nowhere, a black SUV with dark-tinted windows nearly ran him down. He plastered himself against the cold metal of the vehicle. "What the— Hey!"

The SUV kept going. The license plate light was out. Then its taillights disappeared around the corner.

"Michael!" Shay shouted. "Are you okay?"

"I'm fine." If he didn't have a passenger already, he'd be on that driver faster than a hot knife through butter. "Take care, ladies."

During the ride to lock-up, the man in the back fell asleep. At least he was snoring now instead of whining.

That gave Michael a moment to think about why such a fancy vehicle was driving around in his town at this time of night. No high-end clubs. No wealthy neighborhoods. He hoped it wasn't drug dealers.

But they usually tried to keep a low profile. Of course, it could be some uptown addict looking for a connection. Drugs discriminated against nobody.

Maybe after he turned in his passenger and got the paperwork done, he'd cruise around town for a while.

Chapter 14

Jordan padded her way over to the kitchenette while scrolling through the news feeds. No other alerts or any indication of Kyrios leaving Greece for Philadelphia yet. But nothing could calm the nagging wriggle of worry in her gut.

Yes, it could be a coincidence he was coming to Pennsylvania, but with him it was never a straight road. He always planned every step, calculating wins and losses to see which profited him without regard to anyone else.

No sense obsessing. With the kettle plugged in, she pulled out the French press and coffee. The light nutty scent tickled her nose when she scooped the grounds into the glass container. She sat at the bistro table and her phone vibrated. She picked it up.

—*Good morning. Are you awake yet?*—

She pressed send. "Hi, Michael."

"Hey." He yawned.

"What time did you get home?" The kettle whistled, and she poured the water into the press.

"Around seven-thirty."

"What are you doing calling me instead of sleeping?" She chastised him, but her heart leaped that he'd called.

"I wanted to talk to you before you start your day." A dog barked in the background. "Quiet, Forest. I'm on the phone."

"Do you think he understands what that means?" She pushed the plunger down on the press as a smile spread across her face. "Does he answer?"

A whine came over the phone.

"I guess he does."

"I think these hounds are planning a takeover," Michael said. "You need to get me out of here."

"Do you have a plan?" She enjoyed the banter. "A file in a cake, maybe?"

Michael's deep chuckle tickled her insides. "Nah, that's too obvious. They're Shepherds, so probably smarter than us. How about distraction with squirrels while I sneak out and take you to lunch?"

Jordan hesitated. With Kyrios's visit so close, how could she take a chance and endanger not only herself but Michael?

"Jordan?"

"Hang on. I'm seeing what else is happening today." She sucked her bottom lip between her teeth while her heart and head battled—her heart for the win.

"Hmm, I'm fresh out of furry rodents." She sneaked a quick peek at the cabinet. "At least I hope I am. There was a prior tenant here when I moved in who needed eviction after my arrival." She shuddered at the memory of the mouse she'd caught in the humane trap and released outside. "But if you can escape, I'd love to have lunch with you."

"Great." He sounded relieved. "I'll meet you at Heavenly Brew."

"Okay, yes. It's a great place."

"Say, at one o'clock."

"Sounds great." *Please, Lord. Let it be great and*

not a disaster. "If you're late, I'll send someone with tennis balls to distract the doggos while you make a break for it."

She ended the call to Michael's rich laughter.

****

Michael pulled into a parking space about half a block away from the Heavenly Brew café.

The dark-green awning with gold letters created a bright spot on this cloudy day. Snow was in the forecast. The local weather station said they might be in for a big one. Not unusual for the area.

It could snow until April in this part of the country. That would make it a long, busy, and maybe dangerous night.

Car accidents, pedestrian slip-and-falls, it was his duty to respond. What he'd give to be able to stay home, light a fire, and cozy up with the woman he was falling in love with. He flipped up his collar to ward off the chill on his neck. Then he looked up.

His gaze fixed on the figure wearing a bright-red hat in front of the café.

Madeline leaned against the wall. One black-booted heel against the building, her breath drifting from her on the cold air. She tossed a neon-yellow tennis ball up in the air and caught it. When she spotted him, a half-smile appeared on her face, and one eyebrow arched. "Thought I would have to come rescue you after all." She tossed him the ball.

Catching it one-handed, he closed the distance between them. "It was touch and go for a while, but the call of the couch won out."

"I can see the appeal." She pushed off the wall. "Warm blanket, hot chocolate, and a good book. Add a dog or two to the mix—Nirvana."

Michael moved in close. Head tilted to the side, he gazed down into her bedroom eyes. "Hey, any room for me in that scenario?"

"Hmm." She tipped her chin and waggled those elegant brows. "Maybe. But I think I need coffee to make such a serious decision."

"Come on. I never want to get between a woman and her coffee." He reached past her to open the door. Hmm, a black SUV was parked down the street facing their way. The tinted windows prevented him from seeing if anyone was in it.

Madeline noticed his hesitation. "What's wrong?"

"Nothing." He pulled the door open and glanced one last time at the vehicle. Could it be the same one as the previous night?

There were a couple of open tables but none near the window. He'd have liked to have kept an eye on that car.

The previous night it was on the poorer side of town. Today, it was parked in the center city, where they were surrounded by medical facilities and lawyers' offices. A fancy vehicle wouldn't be unusual.

But his inner voice told him it wasn't a coincidence. The drug task force might want to look into it.

"Michael, tell me. What's bothering you? You seem a million miles away."

His attention snapped back to the woman across from him. She perched on the edge of her chair like she was ready to bolt.

"I'm sorry." He reached across the table and covered her hand. "Last night, I had a close call with a black SUV while I was on duty. I guess it shook me more than I realized. When we got here, there was another vehicle resembling it. I'm sure it's nothing."

Madeline pulled back like he'd shocked her. "Did you see who drove it?"

"No."

The waitress approached the table.

"But…"

"I'm sure it's only a coincidence." No sense in winding her up. "I'm going to have the drug task force look into it." He picked up the menu. "I'll have an iced tea with no sweetener. Madeline?"

"Uhm, I'll have the same." She glanced at the waitress. "Oh, hi, Hailey." Then to Michael she explained, "We met near my apartment."

"Nice to meet you." Michael nodded and offered a hand in greeting. "Two jobs, huh?"

"Hi. Student loans." Hailey tucked a stray blonde hair behind her ear and shrugged. "I have several part-time jobs. I work when and where I can."

Hopefully distracted from SUV issues, Madeline relaxed her shoulders. "Hailey went to school to be a music producer and engineer."

The young woman smiled. "What are you having?"

Jordan handed back her menu. "The grilled cheese and tomato soup."

The waitress jotted it down. "Great, and for you?"

"I'll have a BLT," Michael answered. "And chicken noodle if you have it."

Hailey nodded. "Yes, we always have a pot of that on during the winter." She headed to the kitchen to turn in the order.

Madeline's eyes twinkled with mischief from

across the table. "How'd you escape from Forest and Jenny?"

"It was touch and go for a few, but as I said, the seduction of the couch beat their desire to be with me." Good, let's keep the discussion away from the incident the previous night.

"Silly dogs," she drawled.

Michael leaned in closer. "You may want to hang on to that tennis ball."

"Well, I had a backup plan in case that didn't work." She leaned back with a smug smile.

"What was that?"

"Befuddle them with burgers."

Michael snorted. "It may have worked on Forest, but Jenny is a bit more discerning."

"Typical." She chuckled and waved him off. "Girl's got to watch her figure."

"I enjoy your company." Michael grinned at their teasing. He leaned forward, placing his forearms on the table. "You make me wake up and have something to look forward to."

Madeline bit her lower lip and glanced to the side. "Me too."

"I'm glad." His chest warmed. "If I ever push too hard, let me know."

She looked him in the eye. "I'm glad too. And, Michael? So far, I'm pulling as hard as you're pushing."

She slid her hand across the table and turned it palm up in front of his. When his big ole hand engulfed hers, they both sighed.

Lunch arrived, and both dug in, enjoying the comfort food for a few moments in companionable silence. Then she dabbed her mouth with a napkin. "Tell me about your family."

"Not much to tell." His spoon clinked down into the empty bowl. "I'm an only child. My mom died a few years ago."

"I'm sorry." Madeline touched his hand again.

It was something he could get used to.

"What about your dad?"

"Never knew him." He had a picture of his parents in his wallet. "They met when he separated from his wife. Before mom could tell him she was pregnant, he'd reconciled.

"That's tough." Madeline's brow wrinkled. "She never told him?"

"We did okay." He shrugged. "Mom had a good job, so we didn't struggle. She told me she didn't want to be the other woman. Also, she'd been shuttled between her parents after they'd divorced and didn't want to share me."

"She sounds amazing."

He nodded. "And if she loved him, he must have been an okay kind of guy."

"And she never found anyone else?"

Michael swallowed hard. "No. I think he was the love of her life. Sometimes I'd hear her crying after I went to bed. One night I went to her. Told her it would be all right."

"Oh, Michael." Moisture gathered in her eyes.

He nodded, swallowing back his own tears. "She said I was the gift he gave her and that she'd be fine. Said it was never meant to be." Was this why he'd always hesitated? Why he always picked the wrong woman? The fear of being hurt and abandoned like his mother was?

"But now you're alone."

"No." He shook his head and reached across the table to swipe away an escaping teardrop from her cheek. "Not anymore."

****

How did he become such a good guy? Time to go fishing. "Why hasn't some woman laid claim to you."

A big cheesy grin appeared, but it didn't reach his eyes. "Because I was waiting for you."

"Hmm, I sense a story." Jordan took a bite of her super-gooey cheddar on grilled sourdough and nearly moaned.

"That good?"

"Did I make that noise out loud?" Her cheeks heated. "I really thought it was only in my head. Don't deflect. Spill. I told you all my deep dark secrets."

Michael seemed to deflate in his chair.

Uh-oh. Somebody had hurt him. "It's okay. You don't have to get into it here. Some things are too painful to blab about in public."

"No." He sat back in his chair, ignoring his BLT. "Yeah, some of it was painful, but..."

"But, what?" She set her sandwich on the plate and picked up the mug of steaming tomato soup.

"It's just"—he slouched in the chair, rubbing the back of his neck—"I don't want you to think I'm pathetic."

"What? Why?"

Now the tips of his ears were red as her tomato soup. He stared down at his plate while pushing the food around with the fork.

"Michael, you can tell me anything."

140

At the next table, a baby began to fuss. Jordan glanced over at the mom, who was trying to soothe the little guy. Between the child and the clatter of silverware on plates, the noise nearly covered Michael's soft words.

"I'm almost thirty-six years old, and I've never been in a serious relationship."

Her attention turned back to him. "What do you mean?"

"I'm not like most guys." He looked up with a sheepish half-smile. "I never was a player or wanted to be with a lot of women. I mean, I've dated. But if I tried to take a casual relationship to the next level, I was always shot down." He glanced over to where the baby had settled down and was now drinking out of a bottle. "Since I was old enough to understand relationships, all I dreamed of was having my house filled with family. A wife. A couple of kids. Growing old with the woman I love. Seeing our grandchildren playing in our yard."

"There's nothing pathetic about that."

"You should also know something." He hesitated, hoping his words wouldn't affect her relationship with Shay.

"What?"

"Well, I did have a big crush on someone." Sweat beaded on his forehead.

"Did? As in you're over it?" Jordan leaned away. "Wait—I'm not the other woman in this scenario, am I?"

"Good Lord, no." Michael flinched and shifted in his seat. "I'd gotten past it before ever meeting you."

"Who?"

"Shay. But I'm completely over it." The words

tumbled out. "Aden and Shay are together, and it's right. Seeing them as a couple, you just know they were made for each other. And, well, since I first laid eyes on you, I know what I thought I'd felt was nothing compared to how I feel now. About you, I mean."

Jordan reached across the table and grasped his folded hands between hers. If she had any doubts about the truth, him being so flustered quelled it. "Michael, it's okay. Shay is a beautiful woman with a heart of gold. Who wouldn't crush on her?"

Though he nodded, the tension in his face caused an ache in her heart. "How did you get to be such an amazing man?"

"Not so amazing, apparently." He lifted a shoulder and quirked the side of his mouth. Sad brown eyes regarded her over their half-empty plates and glasses.

He laid his heart bare before her, and she had trouble swallowing past the lump in her throat. "Michael, I, for one, think you're not only amazing, but you are handsome, sweet, and a wonderful man. Any woman would be lucky to have you."

A huge sigh escaped him, and he flipped his hands up to lace her fingers with his. "I'm lucky to have found you."

"You know it's been a long time since I was a church-going girl," she whispered. "But I never forget to pray. During the worst of my time with Kyrios, I prayed that one day I would find happiness." Her voice hitched. "That—that I would find someone like you."

Please, God. Please let this somehow work out.

142

Chapter 15

He's coming.

Cold fingers of reality slashed down Jordan's spine. Though she'd known a trip was in the works, when the alert vibrated her phone during rehearsal, she couldn't stop shaking. He wasn't due to come to the States for a few more weeks.

Her chest tightened, and she couldn't draw a breath. Her knees buckled, and she collapsed on Jazz House's stage.

"Madeline!"

Coral's voice sounded like it was in a tunnel.

"Shay, help."

Jordan's vision narrowed onto Shay, who was rushing toward her while tossing her apron over a chair.

"Let me through," the EMT's voice commanded. "Madeline, Madeline. Can you hear me? Are you sick? In pain?"

Finally, a breath wheezed into her lungs along with the scent of Olivia's tea-rose-and-orchid perfume. Jordan rocked back and forth with her arms wrapped around her body. "He doesn't know. He doesn't know."

"Who doesn't know, Madeline?"

Her boss's concerned face came into focus.

"Should I call 911?" one of the men asked.

That jolted Jordan out of her stupor. "No! Don't call. I'll be fine."

Tattooed arms came around and lifted her up and into a chair.

"Thank you, SammyD." Shay backed away to give them room.

"Madeline, what's going on?" Olivia squatted next to her.

Jordan looked up at all the concerned faces and painted on her stage smile. "I'm all right. Just a bit light-headed from not eating."

"No." Olivia grasped her hand. "That was a panic attack. I'm well acquainted with them."

Shay chimed in after taking her pulse. "And who doesn't know what?"

Jordan's heart played a bongo tattoo. "Please."

"Let's go to my office." Olivia stood and towered over her. "We'll have some privacy, and we can talk."

She should just grab her purse and leave. If she grabbed a taxi, she could be home in minutes where a go-bag sat ready. A hard knot tightened in her gut. The backs of her eyes began to burn. She loved these people.

"Madeline, you can trust me." Olivia reached over and stroked Jordan's hair. "I'm your friend."

Jordan nodded, swallowed the lump in her throat, and covered the other woman's hand. "I know."

"I'll get everything back on track out here while you go talk." Shay grabbed her apron from the chair.

Jordan could almost feel the weight of their stares as she allowed Olivia to lead her to the office.

"Okay, everyone." Shay clapped her hands. "Back to work."

Jordan glanced over her shoulder. The staff began to disperse. Their soft whispers were cut off when

Olivia closed the door. While she sat in the red wingback chair, her boss went to the side table and poured water from the cut-glass pitcher.

She placed the glass into Jordan's shaking hands.

"Thank you."

Instead of sitting in the chair behind her desk, Olivia angled the matching wingback to face Jordan. "You're welcome." Then she sat back and stared at her fingernails. "Hmm, life hasn't been all rainbows and unicorns, huh?"

Jordan snorted and shook her head.

"I understand." Olivia sighed. "I'm not sure what's happened, but I get that you're afraid. I am too."

She glanced over at the always-impeccable woman in her cream-colored turtleneck and gray trousers. "You seem pretty put together."

"On the outside." Olivia picked at a cuticle. "You remember your first day? When Michael came in and told us about Kayla getting out of jail?"

Nodding, Jordan said, "I do. You were terrified."

"I still am." Olivia stared past her into the distance. "I still have headaches from her hitting me with a heavy cooking pot. I see someone for panic and anxiety. It worsened after the assault. My therapist says I suffer from PTSD."

"I can understand that." *Where was this going?*

"I knew you would." Olivia looked directly at her now. "That's why I believe you know how important family and friends are to recovery."

Tears welled in her eyes. "I do."

"We're friends, right?"

A sob caught in her throat. "Yes."

"Then, let me help."

The tears overflowed and flooded Jordan's cheeks. "I don't want to leave, but if I don't, you all may be in danger."

A half-hour later, Jordan was exhausted from the telling. "Now do you see? I have to say goodbye."

"No." Olivia now paced the room in the House family way. Several times she touched the side of her head almost identical to the way Jordan touched hers.

"But Olivia, I can't stay and expose you all to Kyrios's threat."

"We can't live our lives in fear." Olivia paused and leaned on her desk. "Neither of us. I know a great lawyer. She'll help us figure out what to do.

****

Michael glanced over as the grandfather clock pinged the quarter-hour when he returned from a run with the dogs. The gleaming mahogany timepiece had been one of his mother's favorite possessions. One she'd inherited from her grandparents.

He headed to the kitchen and made sure the fur-faces had fresh water before trotting upstairs. Finishing the quick shower, he then stood in front of the mirror to shave with the towel wrapped around his waist. Was that a gray hair? Geez, when did he start getting grays? He checked the rest of his head before going to the closet and pulling a fresh uniform.

Navy pants first and a blue T-shirt, followed by strapping on his body armor, before zipping up the light-blue shirt and lacing his black boots. The utility belt he would carry to the station. That sucker added another twenty pounds and was clunky to get in and out of the truck with. It held a flashlight, weapon, extra ammo, radio, pepper spray, rubber gloves. The only other things he needed were grappling hooks and a couple of other gadgets, then he'd feel like a caped crusader.

Michael slung it over his shoulder before tucking his sunglasses into the neck of his shirt. While he trotted down the stairs, the clock bonged the hour. He'd better get a move on. "You guys behave and watch the house."

Forest snored from where he was stretched out on the couch.

"It's all on you, Jenny."

She wagged her tail and followed him to the door.

Michael bent and gave her a quick kiss on the head.

Twenty minutes later, the officer on the door buzzed him through. "Hey, Machau. What's doin'? You're early."

"Not much." The guy didn't really want to know. Most people really didn't. "Early meeting with Romano."

"Good luck. She just chewed out another new-boot."

"Well, they have to learn." Michael continued past, waving to a few others before rapping on the door to the sarge's office.

"Come in."

He lifted an eyebrow at the woman leafing through a pile of papers scowling and mumbling, "Of all the dimwitted, lamebrained—"

"Problems, Sarge?"

"Who taught them to write reports like this?" She glared across the room. "Details. Don't they know details are what makes the case?"

"Maybe make it one of the in-service classes."

"Listen to this." She pulled one of the papers. "*Saw drunk. Arrested same.*"

Michael ran a hand over his face to cover the smile threatening to appear. He didn't want to make her angrier. "Definitely in-service."

She tossed the paper back on the desk, took a deep breath, and collected herself. "I spoke to my connections at the Bureau."

"Great." Michael sat across from her. "Before we talk about that, I want to fill you in on something else."

Alyssa pulled her glasses down and peered over the frames. "Something more important?"

"In our own backyard. I've got a feeling, and it's not a good one." He scratched his forehead. "There's a big black SUV I've spotted in different places around town. I haven't been able to grab a tag number. It's either flying by or parked the wrong way." In Pennsylvania, the only license plate was on the back. "I'm concerned about drug dealing."

The sergeant nodded. "You may be onto something. I received a call not long ago. DEA, the Drug Enforcement Agency, was sending in some undercover people. It seems like an international drug cartel has been spreading up from the city. They're hoping to crack the case."

"That would explain it." He leaned forward. "Do you know who the agents are?"

"We never know." She tapped a short, manicured nail on the desktop. "When they go deep undercover, the fewer with information on their identity, the less chance of exposure."

"Makes sense." Michael released a puff of air. "Hard to believe our little town is now on the DEA's radar."

"Slate Quarry isn't little anymore." She rubbed her temple. "Crime is like a goldfish. The bigger the tank, the bigger the fish. Speaking of big fish, the shark stirring up your water is bad news."

"Yeah, he is. He's been suspected of many different crimes, but none of them stick."

Alyssa pulled off her glasses and began polishing the lenses. "And your particular victim is the only one who ever got away and lived to be able to talk about them."

"For now." Acid churned in his gut. "What did your connection say?"

"For her to lay low a bit more. Michael—" She frowned at him and shook her head. "—if they can gather enough charges against him, she may have to go into witness protection. Your girlfriend may be the one who finally takes him down. If he finds her…"

Michael leaped to his feet. "He won't."

****

After a nine-hour flight from Athens, the private jet landed at a small exclusive airport outside of Philadelphia.

Kyrios hated flying. It put him in a foul mood. No, a fouler mood.

Outside the window, beyond the fence, reporters jostled with local businesspeople and politicians.

Kyrios sat and made them wait while he checked messages. Okay, enough time. He sneered. "Let's get this over with."

Surrounded by bodyguards, he left the plane and pasted on a fake smile. Americans liked people who smiled. They trusted them.

"Mr. Vasilakis, welcome to the US and the City of Brotherly Love," an aide to the mayor prattled on. "The mayor will join us at the restaurant."

Kyrios spent some time on the way into the terminal glad-handing the politicos allowed inside the fence.

Inside, at Customs, there was a pretense of screening him for entry into the country after bypassing the lines of other commuters waiting for their turn. The abbreviated process took bare minutes. And why not? He was bringing business and mutual prosperity to the city. They understood how powerful he was and respected him.

He smiled broader when they left the building.

Police cleared the way to a waiting limousine.

Reporters shouted questions from behind a roped-off barricade.

He gave them rehearsed answers, then he waved and got into the car. When the door closed, he cursed the fools. He barked at Tito, "Go."

Tito banged on the glass separating them from the front.

The driver pulled out into traffic. Moments earlier, the pasty-faced man had taken one look at Kyrios's huge, bald guard and crossed himself.

Tito was intimidating before the incident at Lunae Lucem. But now, scars slashed across his face. The man was a gargoyle.

It pleased Kyrios.

Traffic was heavy, and it took longer to get to the restaurant than anticipated.

When it began to drizzle, he stared out at the cold, miserable rain. It reflected his mood.

"We're here, Kyrie."

The limousine came to a halt, and Kyrios glanced at the driver who darted to open the sedan's door.

Tito led the way up the red carpet under a black-and-gold awing.

The Philadelphia Grand Hotel and Restaurant was world-renowned for elegance and food. So far, it was the only thing that didn't disappoint.

Security stood to the side and held back several photographers and reporters from accosting them.

The Pershing-hatted doorman in a navy-blue uniform opened the way into the cavernous lobby.

Black-and-white marble tiles with silver accents gave the room an art-deco feel.

This, too, pleased him. Maybe he would buy this hotel.

"Mr. Vasilakis, welcome." A besuited man with highly polished black shoes approached. "I am James Tolman, head concierge."

Tito stepped between them and took the proffered card.

Tolman blanched and turned sharply. "Gentlemen, this way."

Their shoes clicked on the harlequin-colored floors.

"Are my hosts here?" Kyrios's lip curled as he waved off another sycophant.

"Yes, sir. They're all seated and awaiting your arrival." The man opened the restaurant door and stepped to the side, giving Kyrios a slight bow. "Enjoy your stay. If you need anything, the Philadelphia Grand Hotel and Restaurant is at your service."

"Good."

Tito brushed by him and surveyed the room. Since

the attack at Lunae Lucem, his personal security was never left to someone else.

A tall, black-haired woman approached, but his guard stopped her.

"Excuse me. I'm Kayla, the hostess here." Her beautiful face pinched at the bodyguard's interference. Then she glanced past Tito, and a slim brow rose when she spotted him. "I've been assigned to see to Mr. Vasilakis's needs."

Kyrios laid a hand on Tito's shoulder. "It's all right. The lovely Kayla means no harm."

Tito stepped to the side, allowing him to pass.

The woman stuck her chin out and gave his bodyguard a curt nod before turning her attention back to him. She ran an assessing gaze down over his clothing, pausing on his handmade Italian loafers. When her attention returned to his face, she stood straighter, thrusting her chest toward him. A long red fingernail traced the vee of her matching sheath dress. "It's quite all right. He only startled me."

"Come, beautiful Kayla." Kyrios closed the distance between them. "Show me to my hosts."

"Of course, sir. This way, please."

When he placed his hand on her lower back, she leaned in toward him, giving a sideways glance. "An important man like you should never be kept waiting."

"A woman who understands." An opportunistic female. Excellent. "I will not be too long. If I am not too bold, would you have dinner with me later? What time do your duties end?"

"I can be finished whenever you like." The red fingernail now trailed down his arm.

"Tito," he turned to the bodyguard. "Miss Kayla

will be joining me for a late supper. What is my room?"

"The penthouse, of course." Tito's face remained impassive. "I'll see to the arrangements."

Chapter 16

Jordan trailed Olivia up the steps toward the elevator. "I'm not sure this is a good idea."

Olivia stopped and turned to face her. "We're going for a consultation. That's all. You talk to Kate. She'll give you advice."

"What if Kyrios finds out?" Jordan gripped the handrail until her knuckles hurt. "If he has no idea where I am, why send up a signal flare?"

Her friend stepped down even with her and grasped Jordan's shoulder. "You don't have to do this right now. We can turn around and go back home. But what did you tell me you wanted more than anything?"

"To be free," Jordan whispered. "To live life on my terms."

Olivia waited, brown eyes lit with concern. Her gaze was unwavering.

Adrenaline surged, causing Jordan's hands to tingle. The impulse to flee was overwhelming. What to do? Running hadn't made her life much better. Living in fear and always looking over her shoulder. Could she continue to exist like this? Because that's what it would be. Existing. She certainly wasn't living most of the time. And what about her future? There could be none with Michael. If he joined her in a life of lies and secrecy, it would eventually tear them apart.

She lifted her chin and squared her shoulders.

"Let's do this."

"I'm proud of you." Olivia nodded and looped arms with her. "Together. No matter what, I'm here for you."

Side by side, they entered the elevator. Exiting, they continued down the hallway in tandem until reaching a door with *Kate Danielson, Esq.* emblazoned on the frosted glass.

Only then did Olivia release her. "I'm with you." The other woman turned and grasped Jordan's biceps. "But you need to open the door and step through. I'll be right behind you."

Jordan took a deep breath.

Make good choices.

Yes, Mama. She licked her lips, steeled her spine, and turned the knob.

As promised, Olivia followed on her heels. She slid off her coat. "Hello, Charlotte. I'm here with Madeline Cielo for an appointment with Kate."

"Ms. House, so nice to see you again." The woman rose and came around the desk. "Here, let me take your coats. Ms. Danielson is finishing up a conference call and will be right with you."

Jordan shrugged out of her jacket and handed it to the administrative assistant. "Thank you."

Olivia settled into a chair while Jordan examined the licenses, certificates, and diplomas neatly arranged on the dove-gray walls. Prestigious universities and multiple degrees. How was she going to afford a lawyer like this? "Olivia," she whispered. "Money is going to be a problem."

"What kind of problem?"

"An I-have-none kind of problem."

"Don't worry about that now." Olivia folded her hands on her lap. "Kate and I are friends. She'll work something out with us." A mischievous smile appeared. "Maybe you can sing for your solicitor?"

"You're hilarious—not."

The inner door opened, and a tall, lean, African American woman with rare green-colored eyes walked through. "Olivia, it's been too long. Come into my office."

"Kate, thank you for taking us on such short notice." Olivia stood, and they hugged before she introduced Jordan. "This is Madeline, whom I spoke with you about."

The lawyer turned to Jordan. "Madeline Cielo, I've heard wonderful things about your singing. You've made quite an impression on my friend here."

They shook hands and then she and Olivia followed her into the office.

"Thank you. Olivia has also made an impression on me." Jordan turned and faced her friend, a bit choked up. "Her kindness, loyalty, and unconditional love have touched me." Her voice broke off, and she placed her hand over her heart. "I'm sorry, this is very emotional for me."

Kate walked around and sat. She leaned on her elbows and appraised Jordan from across her dark-gray desk. "All right. Olivia told me you need to discuss an overseas divorce and protection. You both know I'm not that kind of lawyer? I deal with criminal law."

"Yes," Olivia answered. "And we're not here for you to start proceedings, but looking for advice with a tricky situation."

Jordan snorted. "Tricky? How about a life-and-death situation?"

The attorney raised her eyebrows. "Tell me what this is about. Whose life and death?"

"Mostly mine," Jordan murmured. "But I'm also concerned about those around me, like Olivia."

Kate's gaze shot to Olivia. "What have you gotten yourself into this time, my friend?"

"Madeline has a problem with her husband. She's the best one to tell the story." Olivia reached over to grasp Jordan's hand. "I'm here. Tell her everything. This is all confidential. Nothing leaves the room. Right, Kate?"

"Absolutely."

Jordan took a deep breath and sat up straight in the chair. She lifted her chin and focused on the wall of books behind Kate. "Do you know who Kyrios Vasilakis is?"

The woman nodded, her gaze sharpening. "The businessman. Also, a probable underworld figure."

"My name isn't Madeline." Sweat broke out on her brow even as a chill ran down her spine. "My name is Jordan Vasilakis."

Kate narrowed her eyes at Jordan. "You're dead."

"No," she answered. "I'm alive. For now, anyway."

"Tell me what happened." Kate pulled out a tablet and pen. "Start at the beginning."

"I've always been an entertainer." Jordan crossed and uncrossed her legs. "I loved being the center of attention. It's what got me in this predicament."

"No!" Olivia burst out, leaping to her feet with clenched fists. "That is not what caused this. You're a performer. It's not only what you do but who you are.

What caused this is the evil called Kyrios Vasilakis. Don't you think I've read up on him? This is his doing!" She waved toward the window. "Not you."

Both Jordan and Kate stared at the usually easy-tempered woman they knew.

Olivia's face flushed, and her hands trembled.

"Tell us how you really feel, Liv," Kate drawled.

"I will. That woman is my friend." Olivia pointed at Jordan. "Nearly a sister. The Houses protect those they love. No exception."

Rising from her seat, Jordan crossed to where the emphatic woman stood. She wrapped her arms around Olivia and tugged her into a huge bear hug. "You're such a drama queen," she muttered into Olivia's ear.

They both laughed and returned to their respective chairs, where Jordan continued. "I was young, stupid, and in love."

Both women nodded in understanding.

A short while later, Jordan wrapped it up. "I'm so tired of living in fear. Exhausted from running."

"What do you hope to accomplish in this situation?" Kate set down the pad and pen she'd been making notes with.

"I just want peace." Jordan looked up at the ceiling, blinked her eyes, and sniffled. "To be able to walk out my door without looking for someone in the shadows. To go home and not recon my apartment before settling in. Pick up the pieces of my life and have a family again."

Olivia reached over and covered her hand. "You will."

****

Michael ran a hand over his hair while staring out

the back door, waiting for the dogs to finish patrolling the yard. He hadn't had much time to investigate Vasilakis further. The flu ran rampant through the department, and he'd spent most nights in the patrol car. But what he did learn was terrifying. And Sgt. Romano hadn't heard back from her contacts either.

Kyrios Vasilakis was like a no-stick frying pan. Accusations and legal charges slipped right off him, and most of his accusers ended up getting burned. He could understand why Jordan feared for her life. The man's existence and business were tightly wound in Gordian knots with crime syndicates worldwide.

What the heck could he, a small city cop, do to help the woman he loved? This was too big for him. Sooner or later, if Kyrios figured out Jordan survived, he would hunt her down.

"*Swfft*." He whistled. "Come on, guys, I've got things to do."

Noses to the ground, both dogs ignored him.

Michael reached over to the shelf near the door and grabbed a canister holding a secret weapon. He gave it a shake, then stepped back out of the way.

Forest blew through with Jenny on his heels. Both came to skidding halts.

Michael winced when Forest's less-than-graceful maneuver had him slamming into the fridge, rattling the bottles in the door. "Your head is as hard as a rock," he said when the dog shook off the head thump and sat with his tongue lolling.

After tossing them the beef jerky strips, he gathered up his stuff and headed out to work. It was going to be another long shift. He hadn't seen Jordan in days. Work, sleep, work, sleep. The hamster wheel was spinning.

His barn help parked next to his pickup, and he waved to her. "How's it going, Sherry?"

"Good, Michael," the wiry middle-aged woman answered. "Do you need me to let the dogs out before I go?"

"That would be great." He tossed his duffel onto the back seat. "I'd also appreciate it if you could let them out and feed them for what could be a few days. I'm going to be on duty for I don't know how long. I'll shoot you a text when I'm coming home. There's a storm coming."

"You've got it." She nodded and pushed the wheelbarrow back into the barn.

****

The phone in Kyrios's pocket vibrated around five p.m. About time. He'd tried to focus on his business deals, but thoughts of how close he was to capturing his recalcitrant bride continually interfered. "What?"

Anatole answered without hesitation. "Earlier today, she entered a *kafenio* with a man. My cousin Luka followed him when they left. I stayed with your wife." His voice lowered. "He's *bátsos*—a cop."

Kyrios stubbed out his cigar. These American police were everywhere. So far, he'd been unable to establish more than a minor presence in US law enforcement. It seemed the bigger fish wanted a bigger payoff. And no interest in connections to Kyrios. Fools, how else could he own them. Money? Easy. Reputation tarnished—not so easy. "What else?"

"The club is new," Anatole reported. "There's been no sign of her here yet. But it's early. According to the poster out front, the singer won't start until eight."

"Have you asked around?" Kyrios fumed. She'd found herself another man. "What else do you know?"

Sounds of cars beeping came over the line, followed by a man's voice yelling, "Move it, pal. You're blocking the street."

"*Choíros.*" Anatole cursed. "Sorry, Kyrie. She goes by the name of Madeline Cielo. She started working here earlier this year, shortly after the restaurant opened."

"What else?" Frustration percolated in him like a *briki* on the stovetop. None of this was new. The magazine article said as much. "Could you get nothing more from the people who work there?"

"No, Kyrie." Anatole's voice dropped. "Your instructions were observation. If you need more, you have only to ask."

Kyrios's eyes narrowed. "Soon, I will arrive for a lovely dinner show and surprise my wife."

"Yes, Kyrie," Anatole replied.

"If the policeman gets too close, eliminate him."

"Yes, Kyrie." Anatole sneered on the other end.

"Keep me apprised of anything new." Kyrios ended the call and sprawled on the white sofa. His head pounded. There were so many balls in the air, and he trusted no one.

Two days ago, Interpol had raided one of his most productive warehouses. Millions of dollars' worth of opiates were seized. Luckily for him, the paper trail ended at Sokolov International Enterprises. Grigory was granting him one last favor from the grave.

"Ssss." Air hissed from him. If he hadn't been so distracted by Jordan, the agency wouldn't have gotten that close to the real power behind the scenes. One more grievance added to Jordan's ever-growing tally.

Rap, rap, rap.

"What is it?" he bellowed. Couldn't he have a moment of peace?

"My apologies, Kyrie. But the man you wish to see is with me," Tito answered through the closed door.

Kyrios rubbed his temples and sat up. *Never show weakness.* His father's voice barked in his aching head. Rolling his shoulders, he cracked his neck and rose. The sofa wouldn't do. He moved to the matching club chair. "Enter."

Tito opened the door and blocked the entrance with his body while pulling off his dark glasses. "My apologies again for disturbing you."

"You may show him in." Kyrios waved off the apology.

With a curt nod, his bodyguard retrieved the man from the hallway outside the suite. "This is Brandt."

Kyrios leaned back in the club chair and pushed the framed *No Smoking* sign to the side. He snapped open his personalized walnut traveling smoking kit, then opened the portable humidor. He took his time with the cutter and then lighting the cigar while silently perusing the man who'd entered with Tito. When he'd had a hard time recruiting Stateside personnel, this man, a former *bátsos* with a spotty history of trouble in the ranks, floated to the surface like dross behind others' silver badges.

Brandt's gray-colored eyes were cold and devoid of any emotion. Dirty-blond hair needed a cut, and his suit was not new or expensive. The man fidgeted under his scrutiny.

Kyrios took another puff, let out the smoke, and

asked, "Why are you here?"

Sweat beaded on his forehead, and he turned to Tito. "You told me he wanted temporary security staff while in the U. S."

"You will address me," Kyrios snapped.

The man paled. "My apologies."

He crossed his legs and plucked at the crease. "You work for me. Tito, I'm sure, has explained about loyalty. You know what happens should you cross me in any way?"

"Yes, Mr. Vasilakis." The sweat now ran down in rivulets. "I won't disappoint you."

"Of course you will." Kyrios puffed his cigar. "Everyone always does."

Chapter 17

Jordan checked her phone the moment she woke up. Kyrios's plane had landed yesterday. Videos of him glad-handing the mayor and other bigwigs grated on her nerves. "Careful you don't sell your soul to the devil, fellas."

Unloading to Olivia and then Kate yesterday was exhausting. But she'd slept better the past night now that she wasn't lying to her boss and friend any longer.

Olivia'd promised to keep her secret and was glad Michael knew.

A problem shared is a problem halved. A smile ghosted across Jordan's face when Grandmother's voice ran through her mind. From Ben Franklin's *Poor Richard's Almanac* to the book of Proverbs, and even Erma Bombeck, Grandma always had a quote ready.

Her text alert went off. Speak of the angel. She smiled.

—*Are you up?*—
—*Yes, just now*—
—*Breakfast?*—

She dialed him while turning on the kettle.

"Hey, gorgeous," he responded immediately.

"When did you get home?" Michael had been working long hours due to the flu's impact on the department. "You sound tired."

"A little while ago. I took a shower, and now I

want to see you."

"You should get some sleep." Oh, but she wanted to see him too.

"I'll sleep this afternoon." He sighed. "I have to work again tonight."

Jordan spooned coffee into the French press. "Give me an hour, and I have something to tell you."

"What?" A dog barked in the background. "Forest, wait. He wants to eat. Now."

Jordan laughed. "Feed your dogs. Let me get a shower, and I'll see you at Heavenly Brew. It's not necessarily bad news."

"'K," he grumbled. "I'll wait." There was a cacophony of dog barks as he hung up the call.

Smiling, Jordan poured the water over the grounds and stirred. After placing the plunger in, she went to start the shower. She grumbled as the water chilled her hand, "Maybe an hour and a half by the time the water's hot."

Once showered and dressed, Jordan went through her lockup and security routine. She made sure the card Olivia gave her was in her bag and then trotted down the stairs. She scanned the street up and down before heading for the coffee shop, and more importantly—Michael.

She pulled the zipper up higher on her coat. Dang, but it was raw out today. All around her, people on the street had mists floating up from their breaths. Her nose wrinkled when a diesel bus passed her, its airbrakes whooshing as it came to a stop to let passengers on and off.

In front of the hardware store near the traffic light, bags of ice melt were stacked. A sign in front of them read, *Get it today before the storm.*

"Ugh, I hate ice."

"Me too." A tiny woman, her face resembling a prune, frowned up at her. "My bones can't handle a fall."

Oops, she didn't think she'd said that out loud. Jordan lifted her brow and shrugged. "I don't think mine can either."

The light changed, and Jordan helped the woman tow her red canvas shopping cart across the street. She hefted it up on the opposite curb. "You have bricks in there?"

"No, got my salt, though." She gave Jordan a toothy denture smile. "Thank you, young lady. People often don't take the time to help others anymore. Do you have a husband or boyfriend? I have a grandson who needs a good woman."

"It was my pleasure," she answered. "I do have a boyfriend." Her nerves trilled at saying those words. "He's waiting for me right now. I know you have your salt, but be careful spreading it, okay?"

"I will. And if you're ever looking for a good man, Zack is available. He volunteers with the local ambulance and helps people too." The old lady waved and trundled down the block.

She glanced at her watch. Uh-oh, she would be a little later than an hour.

****

On the way to Heavenly Brew, Michael tuned in to the local news.

Winter's not over yet, folks. The groundhog didn't lie when he predicted six more weeks. There's some bad weather headed our way. Sleet and freezing rain in the higher elevations are expected. Slate Quarry is now in a winter storm advisory with predictions for an upgrade into a warning.

Great. Tonight would be a mess. Michael reached over to switch stations.

In other news. Greek business tycoon, Kyrios Vasilakis, is making his rounds in Philadelphia today.

Michael jerked his hand back.

Tomorrow he will head for Harrisburg by helicopter to meet with the governor. Maybe more of Pennsylvania's economy will benefit from the international magnate's interest.

The back of his neck prickled. Not good. Initial reports were only about the man's interest in Philadelphia because of the port. It seemed now the state was getting more attention. Could this mean he knew Jordan was in Pennsylvania and the Greek was now searching for her?

He pulled into a parking spot near the coffee shop. Jordan wasn't there yet. At least not outside. Michael grabbed his phone.

—I'm here. Where are you?—

Seconds later, his phone vibrated.

—Look in your rearview mirror—

He glanced up. Yep, there she was, all bundled up like a mummy. His insides went gooey. He rolled his eyes. God, he was such a mush.

He climbed out and walked around to the sidewalk. The burning in his chest caught him off guard when she threw her arms around his neck. Michael lifted her and spun them in a circle while kissing her.

Honking from a passing car broke them apart.

When he opened his eyes, a lovely blush in her

cheeks made him want to kiss her again.

****

A few minutes later, they'd settled into what Jordan had begun to think of as their spot, near the window. When Michael had gotten out of his vehicle and came toward her, she couldn't help herself. Not usually one for public displays of affection, she launched herself at him.

Well, at least she wasn't the only one. She recognized the goofy look on his face. She'd seen it on her own in the mirror.

Adam, the waiter, didn't even ask what they wanted to drink but set two steaming mugs of coffee in front of them before pulling a pen and order pad from his green apron. "Good morning."

"Hi, Adam." Michael didn't even glance at the menu. "I'll have my usual."

"Great. One Taylor, egg, and cheese." Adam jotted the order. "And what about you?"

"I think I'll have the pumpkin-spice French toast." She'd tried it once before, and it was amazing.

"I'll be back in a few minutes."

The waiter had barely left when Michael asked, "What do you have to tell me?" Then he scratched his head. "I have something to tell you too."

Jordan opened her bag and pulled out the business card. She passed it over to him. "Olivia gave me this. And yesterday, she went with me to meet her."

Looking up from the card, Michael leaned back, a line between his brows. "Why would Olivia give you Kate Danielson's card?"

"Well." Her tummy churned. "I sort of had a meltdown at work."

His face paled. "Why? Did something happen?"

"Nothing, really." She rubbed her temple. "It's just—I knew he was coming. But the reality of his being here? A whole new level of angst."

"You should've called me." He frowned and reached across the table to cover her hand. "So, you had this meltdown. What else?"

Jordan bit her bottom lip and squinched her face. "I may have told Olivia everything."

"May have?"

"Yeah, well, I did."

"Okay, so the secret isn't so secret any longer." He blew a breath through pursed lips. "Then what happened?"

"Michael." Her eyes filled with tears. "She was unbelievable. Olivia wouldn't hear of me running away."

"Wait!" He reeled back. "You were going to run? Without telling me?"

"Michael, no." She grappled for his hand.

The waiter brought their food, took one look at their expressions, set the plates down, and quickly left.

Even the people at the closest tables gave them the side-eye.

She lowered her voice. "No, it was a knee-jerk reaction."

Though he didn't squeeze her hand, the tension in his wrist and forearm was apparent. She clasped his hand and stroked it. "Believe me. I wasn't thinking straight. I would've contacted you, but Olivia was right. I can't keep running."

"Promise me." His Adam's apple bobbed. "Promise me you won't leave. Give me a chance to make things right."

"I promise."

"Okay, then." His shoulders relaxed a tiny bit. "Tell me the rest."

"Olivia is keeping the secret." She continued to stroke his hand. "Do you know Kate Danielson?"

"Yes, she helped Shay back when things were crazy with Aden's ex-girlfriend, Kayla. Ms. Danielson is smart. An excellent lawyer."

"I only just met her, but I think you're right." She took a sip of coffee. "We talked for about an hour."

"What did she advise you to do?"

"Well, she's not the kind of lawyer I need." She put the cup down. "There are lawyers who specialize in international divorce. And with these special circumstances, it will have to be a specific type of attorney. Right now, Kate wants me to keep my head down. Said to be patient until she gets back to me."

"Sounds like good advice." His stomach growled so loud they both laughed. "What? I haven't eaten since last night."

"I'm starving too." Jordan reluctantly released his hand to spread butter and then pour maple syrup on her French toast. "What did you want to tell me?"

Michael wiped his mouth with the napkin. "Well, now there's two things." He leaned toward her and, in a soft voice, said, "Kyrios isn't staying in Philadelphia."

She gasped with a forkful halfway to her mouth. "He's not coming here, is he?"

"No, he's going to Harrisburg." His jaw ticked. "But I wanted you to be aware he's moving around."

She put her fork back down, her appetite gone.

"The second thing is, I talked with my sergeant

about the situation. She wants us to be patient as well. Alyssa has contacts with government agencies, and as soon as she has information, she'll let me know."

Jordan shifted in the chair, eyes blinking like she was sending a telegraph. "Too many people know, Michael, too many. Maybe I should leave town for a while."

"I get it." Michael raised his hands in a calm-down gesture. He knew better than to say the words *calm down* to a woman. "I really do. But we need more people on our side. Your soon-to-be-ex-husband—" He grimaced. "—is a dangerous man. Sweetheart, we need help."

"I hate this."

I understand." Retaking her trembling hand, he continued, "Running isn't the answer. Ending this is."

****

"*Naí*!" Kyrios growled at yet another interruption. "What is it now?"

"Such a small world we live in," Tito answered in Greek. "Your new girlfriend, she has a boyfriend."

His finger tapped the arm of the chair. "Ahh, not very loyal, then? No real surprise."

"I trust no woman." Tito glanced toward the bedroom where Kayla slept.

"What makes you say small world?"

The bodyguard spoke into the mic on his collar. "Bring him in."

Sounds of scuffling came from the hallway. Tito positioned himself closer to Kyrios, standing next to him as the door opened.

"*Kyon*." Dimitris, another black-suited guard, insulted someone in the hall and then shoved him into the room, where he landed on his knees. He kicked the man in the ribs.

The man grunted at the impact.

Dimitris grabbed him by the hair and lifted his face for Kyrios to see. "Our private detective."

The door behind him opened.

"Kyrios, please. I was sleeping." She gasped.

Kyrios turned and beckoned. "Join us, my dear."

Kayla stopped mid-sentence and froze while tying the belt of her robe. "What is he doing here?"

"As I believe you know, former police officer Brandt is on my payroll, beautiful Kayla." Kyrios patted the arm of the chair. "Come, sit. I think Tito has a story for me. And I certainly have questions for you."

The bodyguard turned a gimlet eye on her.

She usually treated Tito with disdain. Today, however, her pale face turned white, and she eyed him like a serpent in her favorite shoe.

Brandt stopped struggling. At least he had some sense.

"Let me get dressed first." She pasted on a brave face and turned to go back toward the bedroom.

"No," Kyrios barked. "Do as I say." He reached out and jerked her toward him, propping her on the arm of the chair. "Sit. Tell us your story, Tito."

The big man strolled over to the bar and poured a cup of coffee. "As usual, I ran a background check on your new woman."

"I can't believe you ran a check on me." Kayla shrilled and started to stand.

Kyrios forced her back down. "Sit," he growled and then licked his lips as she rubbed at the marks left on her arm. "Continue the story."

"Woman is a"—he struggled for the word—"*Enklematias?*"

"Criminal?" Kyrios laughed. "Darling, you did not tell me this. A fine upstanding gentleman such as myself cannot have such a person as my consort."

"I'm not a criminal," she protested.

Tito filled him in on the activities of the woman who warmed his bed. And the former detective who'd helped her in trying to frame some other female. Nonetheless, he was growing impatient to see where Jordan fit into this. "This is all very enlightening, but where does my wife fit into this?"

"Your wife? How can you marry me if you already have a wife?"

Even Dimitri laughed.

Tito jerked his chin toward Kayla. "She worked in a restaurant called Rock House Grill. Dated one of the owners. Man's sister is manager and part-owner of Jazz House."

A bark of laughter escaped Kyrios. "Tito, you are a man of understatement. Small world indeed."

A plan began to take shape in his mind. People were pawns in his game of life. Though he had many accusations made against him in his time, none had ever taken root. *Because you are smarter than everyone else.*

He puffed on his cigar and nodded at Dimitri.

The next few minutes were filled with grunts and groans peppered with an occasional plea.

When Kayla wailed and ran to crouch in the corner of the room, Kyrios threatened to cut her tongue out.

Brandt and Kayla were fools too. They thought him stupid.

Brandt confessed everything.

Kyrios glanced over at the man on his knees, sporting black eyes with blood dripping from his split lip. "You are no man." He uncrossed his legs, leaned forward, and pointed. "This woman would have cut you off in a second to get at my money."

Kayla cowered in the corner. She'd cried in silence with her hands over her mouth since he threatened to cut out her tongue if she continued to make noise.

"Tito."

"Yes, Kyrie?"

"Kill him." Kyrios plucked at the seam in his trousers. "Then have Anatole find the man's cousin, the restaurant critic, and hold him somewhere until you take Kayla to him."

A squeak came from the corner, drawing his attention. His lip curled. "Do you wish to say something?"

Her head whipped back and forth.

"I didn't think so." He rose from the chair, strolled over to the wet bar, and leaned against it. "You will do what it seems you do best, lovely Kayla. Cause trouble for those in Slate Quarry."

Lifting the glass, he swirled the liquid until the ouzo changed from clear to cloudy. He sipped the licorice-tasting beverage. A smile crept across his face, and he happily popped a bite of tapas from the platter.

He had not risen to his preeminent place in the world by rushing and making rash decisions. As angry as he was, time was his friend. With the patience of a scorpion fish, he would wait for the next couple of days. Not only did he not want any connection to the former policeman's *accident,* but his errant woman also was not a fool.

Jordan would keep track of his movements through the local media. He would lull her into false security. Hide in plain sight. Then, only when he was ready, would he sting with the venom he'd built up for months.

Chapter 18

In the hours since Jordan kissed him goodbye, Michael couldn't believe how much he missed her. The flu was still going around, and he needed to work a double shift. Then he'd slept a few hours before returning to duty.

Did she think about him? He grabbed the doorknob of another shop. Yep, locked up tight. He pulled his collar up and zipped his jacket higher. There'd been a spate of break-ins recently in the business district. He cursed when he slipped on ice between the two buildings and nearly fell. The night was fit for neither man nor beast.

Only another week, and he'd be done with the overnight shift for a while. On top of the usual monotony, interrupted with occasional stupidity, the midnight shift was miserable to be relegated to at this time of year.

Movement down the narrow alley caught his attention. He pulled the flashlight from his utility belt. The bright beam lit up the area.

A bundle of rags near a dumpster moved.

"Who's there?"

No response. He took a few cautious steps closer and loosened the strap to his firearm. When he got closer, he realized it was an old painter's tarp. Gently he nudged the lump under it with his foot. "Hey."

Someone grumbled and rustled, and dirty holey gloves gripped the edge of the tarp. A scraggly face emerged. "What do you want? I'm not bothering anybody."

Homelessness was an issue across the country, but it could be deadly during the winter in Northern Pennsylvania.

"This is no place to be sleeping, my man." Michael squatted down. The smell of alcohol burned his nose. "You think the weather's bad now? It's supposed to sleet later tonight and tomorrow."

"Shelter's full," the man said and then coughed. "Plus, they won't let me keep Mutt."

A black nose poked out at the mention of his name.

"Hey, buddy." Michael extended his hand, and the dog gave it a sniff and lick. "I bet you'd like a warm place too."

"Nope." The man gripped the tarp like it was a lifeline. "Not getting separated. Mutt needs me. Don't you, boy?"

As if he understood, Mutt whined and ducked back under the tarp.

"I'm not going to let you get separated." Michael stood up and yanked his wallet out. He riffled through and found the card he wanted. "Here, look at this. There's a church not far from here that runs a temporary shelter that is pet-friendly. They'll even have a vet check the pup out and give it vaccines if needed."

The old guy stared at the card. "I can't read."

"Then I guess you'll have to trust me."

He peered with rheumy eyes at Michael. "You got a dog?"

"Sure do." He pulled out a picture of Forest and

Jenny and handed it over. "Rescued them a few years ago. I wouldn't let anyone separate us either.

The guy stuck his head under the tarp, and Michael stiffened.

"What do you think, Mutt?"

Michael fought the laughter threatening when he realized the man was consulting the dog.

A whine and yip later, they both wrestled to come out from under the tarp.

Michael gave them a hand. When they were all untangled, he asked, "What's your name?"

"Jim. Jim Crawford." He extended a hand. "And I wasn't always like this."

"No worries, man." Michael helped gather up his meager belongings. "Sometimes, stuff happens."

He hefted a heavy bag and peeked inside. It was full of canned dog food. "Let's get you and Mutt somewhere warm."

When they were loaded into his car, Michael radioed dispatch. "Officer Machau to dispatch. I'm transporting a civilian to St. Francis shelter. Can you call them and advise one male, one canine."

"10-4 Machau," Shirley, the dispatcher, replied.

An hour later, Jim and Mutt were settled in.

Michael was thankful for shelters that opened their doors for pets. Those two had a special bond. If places like St. Francis didn't exist, someone like Jim could die before abandoning his pet.

The sleet was coming down now.

Michael shook the ice from his head and got into the car. He keyed the mic. "Machau back in service."

"10-4. Be safe out there, officer." Shirley was like a hen, and the cops her chicks.

"Will do, Shirley." He pulled out and headed toward the city center.

Other voices on the radio squawked about disabled vehicles and a couple of fender benders. Alex Vasquez griped on the private channel about the knuckleheads who were out driving around.

The windshield wipers had a hard time keeping up.

Michael turned the defroster up higher. He squinted through the windshield at the car flashers on the side of the road. Was someone up ahead trying to flag him down? Yep.

After pulling his hat and gloves back on, he flipped the red-and-blue light-bar switch. He couldn't catch a break tonight. "Time to get wet and cold."

He made it to the front of his cruiser when out of nowhere came a black SUV.

"Look out, man," shouted the stranded motorist.

Michael tried to scramble out of the way but couldn't get traction. His life didn't flash by in slow motion, as they said. The only thing he experienced was a vision of a beauty with big brown eyes and a dazzling smile, and then a profound sense of regret.

Chapter 19

Jordan shifted on the beige vinyl chair at the side of Michael's hospital bed.

The monitors beeped, and liquid dripped from the IV bags into the tubing attached to him. The hiss from the automatic blood pressure cuff, periodically inflating, joined in.

She looked at her watch. Had it only been three hours since she'd gotten the call? Only an hour since they'd transferred him from the recovery room to ICU? "Dear God. It's me. Jordan. I know I haven't spoken to you in a long time." Her hand gripped Michael's through the railing. "I'm sorry. I'm sorry for everything. But please don't punish Michael for the bad choices I've made."

Shay wrapped her arms around Jordan from behind. "Michael wanted us to call you. He regained consciousness for a moment at the scene."

Jordan nodded.

"He wanted to give you access to him, so he signed your name as an emergency contact." Shay had been one of the EMTs to respond to the accident scene.

"Do Olivia and Aden know?" Jordan could barely get the words out. "What about tomorrow? I mean tonight. I'm supposed to work, but I won't leave him."

"I called them. They're on the way. It's still icy." Shay let her go and went to the other side of the ICU bed. "Aden's business partner, Eli, is going to Jazz House. His wife Margaret will stay at Rock House until they close. The CorSams will handle the entertainment. Just worry about you and Michael."

"His vital signs have stabilized, but the doctor said he is still critical." Jordan fought back her tears. "He said Michael should recover, but nothing is one hundred percent."

Shay nodded. "That's good news. David, Olivia's husband, talked to Dr. Amara Belo. She's the emergency room doctor who said the same thing. They aren't allowed to say a hundred percent. Nothing in life is."

David Errapel was the surgeon who'd operated on Aden last year. Jordan was glad they had an ally at the hospital.

The radio at Shay's side went off. Another call was coming in. The woman looked at Jordan. "I'll get someone to cover."

"No. Go." Jordan appreciated her friend's willingness to stay. "You can't do anything here. Out there, you can. There are so many of Michael's people here. I'll be fine."

In the hours since the surgery to relieve pressure on his brain, a parade of people were in and out of the surgical waiting room. And now, only certain people had access.

Jordan thought it was only allowed because they were police. There was a special bond between the hospital and police staff.

"Okay, I'll check in with you later." Shay kissed the top of Jordan's head. "When I came in, I heard you saying sorry to God. You know Eli had a conversation with Aden after his accident. I'd like you to know what he said to him about God, events, and punishment."

She sniffled. "What?"

"Eli says He is a God of love." Shay skirted the bed and walked to the glass door. "I don't know what you think you did to cause something to happen to Michael, but this wasn't due to some punitive, vengeful deity. People make choices—good and bad ones. There are repercussions from those choices. But Eli says He's a second-chance God who uses times like this to work things out in people's lives. Just something to think about."

"Shay?"

The other woman paused and looked over her shoulder.

"Thank you. My mom and grandma believe that too."

"The ice is bad. It was an accident. You take care."

Jordan nodded, and Shay walked out, but she couldn't help the flash of doubt. The man who Michael stopped to help told the police the black SUV never slowed, and it looked like they'd been heading right for Michael.

No sooner had the door slid closed than it reopened.

"I have to go. We're going to track down the person responsible. If you need anything, you call me." Lieutenant Morgan handed her a card. "Anytime."

Michael's supervisor arrived at the hospital during the surgery. At that time, he'd said there was as yet no word on the vehicle that ran Michael down.

Another of Michael's fellow officers waiting during the surgery—Vasquez—told her that a BOLO was issued. When she told him she didn't know what that meant, he explained, "It used to be called an all-points bulletin, but now we use *be on the lookout* instead. BOLO is an acronym."

Something must have happened. "Did they find the car that hit Michael?"

"Yes." Morgan ran a hand over his hair. "Abandoned down by the train tracks. It was reported stolen a few days ago near Philadelphia. We now have a clue. And soon, we'll have the driver." He turned and left.

Through the glass wall, several others nodded at her and followed him.

The struggle to maintain her secret fought with telling Morgan about her past. If it were Kyrios, she'd be on the run again and probably soon dead. But if it indeed was a coincidence? Opening her mouth might do more harm than good. Maybe she should ask the sergeant.

Alexander Vasquez, a now-familiar face, poked his head in the room. "Most everyone is leaving."

"Move it, rookie." Sergeant Romano pushed past him. "The hospital is kicking us out. They said there are too many of us here."

Alex and the sergeant had arrived with what Jordan thought must have been most of the force. Though grateful for the support, at this point, she just wanted to be left alone with Michael.

"Vasquez, step outside a minute."

He nodded and exited the room.

"Ms. Cielo, we're going to track down the person responsible." Romano walked to the bed, her mouth tight and eyebrows drawn. "I promise you."

"Thank you, Sergeant Romano." Jordan twisted her hands in her lap. She bit her lip, then said in a hushed tone, "Michael told me he'd spoken to you. About my—um—situation."

"He did." Romano shook her head. "I'm sorry for all that's happened to you. So you know there's a strong possibility Officer Machau was targeted, right?"

Jordan swallowed the bile in the back of her throat and nodded. "I want to believe it's an accident."

"As do I." The sergeant walked around the bed and stooped down next to her. "This is a tricky situation. I have to let my superior, Lt. Morgan, know. I promise we'll do our best to keep you safe."

"I understand." Her whole body began to tremble.

"Jordan." Romano lowered her voice and used her real name, then grasped her hands. "Michael is family to us. That means you are too. We always take care of our family."

Tears slid down Jordan's cheeks. "Thank you. You sound like my boss Olivia House."

"Well then, you have a lot of family around you." The sergeant reached into her back pocket and pulled out a black wallet. "Oh, and before I forget. This is Michael's. Give it to him when he wakes up."

The woman didn't say if. She said when. "Thank you. I will."

"Madeline." Romano rose and stood with shoulders back, and chin held high. "He will recover." Then she turned like a soldier during drills and walked out.

No wonder she was a sergeant. The woman instilled confidence and determination.

Jordan looked at the black leather wallet. Who was his emergency contact before he named her? His mother was gone. There was no father. Maybe an aunt or uncle? A cousin? She flipped open the black leather. His gold badge shone like a beacon in the gloom of the room. She ran her finger over it. His ID was on the opposite side, Michael's handsome face looking directly at the camera. Her breath hitched.

She flipped the separator and smiled at the picture of Forest and Jenny. Someone needed to visit the house. Maybe Aden would. The dogs knew him. She turned the plastic sleeve, and her breath caught in her chest.

"Oh my God, Michael." Stunned, she stared at the man in the bed, then back at the picture of Michael's mom. The smiling dark-haired woman was tucked under the arm of a familiar face. She'd held a similar photo during girls' night out at Olivia's condo. Almost in an identical pose. Aden and Olivia's mother with the same man.

The mystery of Michael's missing father was now solved.

Chapter 20

Two days.

Jordan stood, leaning her forehead against the cold windowpane. The longest two days of her life.

Michael hadn't even twitched the entire time.

Swishing noise from the ICU door sliding open made her turn.

"Good morning." Olivia's husband, David, stopped in regularly. His brown eyes focused on her. "How are you?"

"He hasn't woken up." Jordan swallowed hard. "Why hasn't he?"

"It's not unusual." David walked up to the bed, leaned over, and shone a penlight in Michael's eyes. "Madeline, all his vital signs have improved. He is no longer critical. Head injuries improve in baby steps."

"I understand that." She sniffled and wrapped her arms around her waist. "I miss him."

"Give it time." David straightened, pushing a lock of sandy-blond hair off his face. "You have to take care of yourself too. When was the last time you went home?"

"I haven't." Her jaw set. "And I won't. Not until he opens his eyes."

David gave her a sad smile. "I get it. Talk to him. He can hear your voice. It helps patients in comas."

After the man left, she returned to her chair near

the hospital bed. The blanket under her hand and arm was scratchy when she reached for Michael's hand. His skin was cool. She gave it a gentle squeeze. "I won't leave you, so you have to wake up. Aden and the woman who helps with the horses are taking care of your dogs. The trio is covering my absence at Jazz House. And Michael, I have something important to tell you. I need to tell *you* first, but I can't sit on this for a long time. It wouldn't be fair to Olivia and Aden."

What else was there to say? Talking about the weather was stupid. She didn't know sports. Maybe she could give him a reason to wake up. "David says you can hear me." The words caught in her throat. "I never told you much about my family. I lost my dad when I was six."

The beeping of the monitors and hissing of the automatic blood pressure machine were the only response.

But, talk to him, they'd said. "My mom is gorgeous." She pulled her arms back, set them on the top rail, and rested her chin. "That side of the family has a long history in Louisiana. She runs a boutique there."

Jordan grew up around all the beautiful clothes and textiles that came from local artists and designers as well as from South America.

"Mom heard about a start-up company in Brazil that turned out amazing work." Jordan reached through the rails and picked up Michael's hand. "Grandma watched the business while mom left for a trip to check things out in São Paulo.

Closing her eyes, Jordan imagined her mother as the vibrant young woman she barely remembered, not the sad echo of one since last she saw her.

"People say I have my dad's smile and my mother's eyes." The words poured out. "He was a Brazilian man who ran an import-export business. They met. It was love at first sight, and when she had to return to the States, he followed."

One day, while Jordan sat at her mother's sewing machine learning to make a straight seam, her mother wistfully told her about the whirlwind romance and marriage.

"I was born shortly after their third anniversary." Jordan looked up and stared off into the distance at nothing. "I remember him. He was tall and lighter-skinned than my mother. Oh, and his laugh. It made me so happy."

"They took a second honeymoon when I was six." She turned Michael's hand over and rubbed his callouses from working around the house. She studied the lines crisscrossing. Which was his lifeline? "It was a boating accident. He died of a head injury."

Pausing to collect herself, she pinched the bridge of her nose. "Mom was never the same after that. And, Michael, I won't be either. I love you too much to get over losing you."

Breath caught in her chest. She froze. Did he just squeeze her hand? "Michael, can you hear me? If you can, please squeeze my hand again."

One second. Two. She hitched a breath. There it was. Light, but not just a reflex. His thumb brushed over the top of her hand. Pulling their hands to her lips, she kissed the back of his. "Michael."

His lids fluttered, then blinked a few times. "Love you too, Mad…"

Tears streamed down her face. "Oh, Michael."

Jordan pressed the nurse's call button.

****

Over the next couple of days, Michael's alertness levels grew longer and more focused.

"Your pupils are equal and reactive. All your vital signs are steady, and the last MRI showed improvement." Dr. Morris, the staff neurologist, clicked off the penlight he'd used to check Michael's eyes. "I don't see why we can't look at a release day later this week."

"This weekend?" Michael blinked. "That's great."

The doctor paused and glanced up from the electronic chart. "You're making good progress, but there are some limitations and conditions to a discharge."

Michael frowned, and the movement caused his stitches to pull. He touched the bandage swathing his head. "What kind of conditions?"

A light knock at the door heralded Jordan's arrival. This time instead of a frown pulling at his sutures, the smile cracking his mug at the sight of her beautiful face did. *Ouch.* "Hi."

"Hi." She glanced at the doctor. "Should I come back?"

"That's up to my patient." The doc eyed the bag with the Heavenly Brews logo in her hand. "That's not coffee, is it?"

"Nope, herbal tea." She set it on the bed tray. "I'll step out until you're done."

"No." Michael stopped her. "I'd like you to stay."

Jordan leaned against the bedside rail and grasped his hand. "What's going on?"

"Officer Machau and I are discussing his possible release and the do's and don'ts of going home."

Jordan's gaze shot to him. "You're going home! That's wonderful."

"Settle down, you two." Dr. Morris sighed. "Now listen. There's no driving. No heavy lifting. You should avoid stairs for a bit." The man glanced again at Michael's record. "According to my notes, you live alone, yes?"

"Yes," Michael said. "Well, I have two dogs and horses."

"I recommend you have someone stay with you for a while." He tapped on the tablet in his hands. "You'll need assistance. Bending over and getting out of bed or a chair may cause dizziness. We can't have you falling or doing things that will raise your blood pressure."

"Don't worry, Dr. Morris." Jordan peered at Michael. "If it's okay with Michael, I'll stay with him and won't let anything happen."

"Thank you," Michael said. The corner of his mouth quirked.

"What?"

"Remember when you said you could get used to country living, and I replied, 'I hope so'?"

A bark of laughter burst from her. "Pretty extreme tactics."

"Desperate times call for desperate measures." His voice lowered, and he tugged her hand. "I'm a most desperate man."

"Michael," she whispered and bent over the bedrail closer to him.

A throat cleared from across the room. "Oh, and there will be none of *that* until you're cleared medically.

Jordan reeled back with her hand to her cheek. "Sorry."

"Killjoy," Michael muttered.

****

Friday afternoon, Jordan slid behind the wheel of Michael's truck. She'd used his pickup to get around while he was in the hospital. It facilitated traveling back and forth to take care of the dogs and make sure Sherry, the barn help, knew Michael wasn't available and if anything came up to contact Jordan.

"My new-to-me car will be registered soon, but I have to say, I like the truck." She never considered herself a pickup kind of girl. Michael looked handsome and sexy behind the wheel, but she was surprised at how much she liked driving it. Glancing over at him, she grinned. "Maybe I should get a cowgirl hat and boots. I think I can rock this country girl thing."

"Nah, I like my jazz woman." He returned her smile. "Thank you for doing this for me."

She fired up the engine, put it in gear, and pulled out of the parking spot. "I want to help. It's not a hardship doing things for those you care about. And I care about you, Michael."

"Still, it never hurts to say thank you." He reached over the center console and cupped the back of her neck. "Our relationship is still pretty new, and I don't want you to reconsider. It's tough to be a cop's partner."

"I'm a tough woman." She was surprised. After her marriage to Kyrios, she felt anything but tough. But now, no longer under his influence and with allies, especially Michael, she felt vitalized, like she could do anything.

Soon they turned off the highway onto the road leading to his house. "Let me go in and put the dogs out in the yard. When you're settled, we'll bring them in."

"Sounds like a good plan." His voice shook a bit.

The ride was a little bumpy. Potholes in Pennsylvania were notorious.

After pulling into the driveway, Jordan put the vehicle in park and turned to face him. Her heart leaped. "You're very pale. Are you okay? Should I take you back?"

"No, I'm just a little carsick." His Adam's apple bobbed, and a bead of sweat trickled at his temple. "Go ahead. I'll be fine."

Chapter 21

Michael woke in the brown leather recliner. As much as he'd wanted to lie down and sleep, the doctor told him to keep his head elevated.

The dogs had finally settled down, and Forest lay in front of the fire Jordan had built.

As if they knew something was wrong with him, neither had jumped on him or tried to climb onto the chair. But they'd paced the floor, whining.

Jenny lay on the floor by him, her soft russet-colored eyes watchful.

Moving his head slowly to avoid pain, he looked around the room. No sign of Jordan. Then a whistle from the teakettle came from the kitchen.

A few minutes later, dressed in black yoga pants and one of his green-flannel shirts, she carried two steaming mugs into the living room.

A light fruity scent tickled his nose. "That smells good." He straightened up in the chair and beamed at her. She looked right at home in his place. "What is it?"

With a smile, she handed him a cup. "I noticed you were moving around and figured when you woke up, you'd like something. It's blueberry and lavender herbal tea. I read that berry is good for inflammation, and lavender is calming."

He took a sip. "It's good. Thank you."

She walked over, sat on the edge of the couch, and

placed her cup on the coffee table. With arms resting on her lap and hands clasped, a pensive expression washed across her face. "We need to talk. I have to tell you something, and it's important."

Lavender might have been calming, but it did nothing to stop the clench in his gut at the words *we need to talk*. That was woman code for trouble was going to hit the fan.

"What's wrong?" He managed to sound calmer than he felt. "Is it Kyrios?"

"No." She turned her head to look at him. "It's not necessarily bad. But possibly life-altering. I wanted to wait until you were stronger, but as your accident showed, tomorrow isn't guaranteed."

Michael pinched the bridge of his nose. "Are you breaking up with me? I'm sorry. I know you didn't sign on to be my nurse and aide, but..."

"No," she blurted and hurried over to him. Squatting next to the chair, she gathered up his hand. "Don't you even consider feeling bad or guilty about this. Accidents happen, and when you love someone, you care for them."

He focused on her face. Sincerity and honesty were emblazoned in her eyes. His heart started banging. "You love me?"

She reached up with a hand and cupped his cheek. "You probably don't remember the first time I said it. You were in and out of consciousness. You said you loved me too."

He took a deep breath. "I do. I think from the moment I saw you, there was something."

Leaning back on her heels, she let go of his hand. "I really need to tell you this."

"As long as it's not goodbye, I'm listening."

Jordan stood and walked over to the desk in the corner. She returned with his wallet. "When you were in the hospital, Sgt. Romano gave me this for safekeeping. I flipped it open and saw a picture of your mom, and I'm guessing your dad?"

He nodded. "Yeah, she was pregnant with me. They looked happy together, and it's the only thing I have of him."

"Michael?" Jordan sat on the edge of the coffee table. "When we had our girls' night at Olivia's—" She bit her lip. "—there was a picture of her and Aden's mom and dad."

The hair on his neck stood up.

"It was the same man."

The grandfather clocked ticked in the background, louder in the silence.

Maybe he was still asleep. Thoughts of the pair flittered through his mind. How quickly they'd bonded. How comfortable they were to be with. Even the same brown eyes. Michael licked his lips. "You're sure?"

"Not a doubt about it."

Michael retracted the footrest and slowly pushed out of the recliner. He walked to the sliding glass door and stared out with hands on his hips.

Forest whined.

Thoughts ran rampant. How? Why? What would he do? "Do they know? Have you told them?"

"No." Her voice was soft. "I wanted to tell you first."

When he turned back to Jordan, the back of his eyes were hot with unshed tears.

Jenny sat on the floor next to Jordan with her paw

on the compassionate woman's lap.

"I have a brother and sister." He choked the words out past the lump in his throat.

Jordan gently lifted the paw off and got up. She walked over to Michael and wrapped her arms around his waist. Laying her head against his chest, she whispered, "Yes, you do."

****

When his body eased, she said, "I'll call them for you. If you like?"

"That would be great." Michael nodded. "Would you mind if I had a few minutes to wrap my brain around this? I'd like to go into the yard. I've missed it."

Jordan helped him don the navy jacket. "Take a walk, a slow walk, around the backyard. Get your thoughts together."

"Go ahead and call them. I need to get this done." He ran a hand over his head and winced. "I need to see how they react. Whether they'll accept me."

Jordan closed the door but kept a close eye on Michael.

The doctors recommended an easy walk, and he needed some time alone to come to terms with having a family.

When he reached the back of the yard near the pasture, he leaned against the railing, not moving for long minutes.

His horses grazed on scant new grass growing beyond the fence.

The dogs, who'd followed him, milled about sniffing.

The pastoral scene out back didn't calm her spirit as she expected it would.

Forest jumped and rested his paws on the top too.

She snorted when the big German Shepherd gave Michael a bright-green tennis ball, knowing how slobbery it would be.

But Michael was a champ. He patted the dog, took the ball, and tossed it over his shoulder.

Her heart ached for him. And for herself. If things went smoothly with Aden and Olivia, he would have a family again. Her future was still unknown.

Grandma's voice whispered through her head, quoting a psalm, *Why am I discouraged? Why is my heart so sad? I will put my hope in God!*

Jordan sighed and pulled out her cell. "Okay, Grandma. Message received—no more wallowing." She tapped Olivia's contact and waited for her to answer.

"Hey, Madeline," Olivia answered on the third ring. "How's Michael? Do you need anything?"

"Um, he's good. Tired."

"To be expected. I was the same when I was recovering, and my head wound wasn't nearly as bad."

Olivia's injury indeed hadn't been as severe, and she still had headaches. Hopefully, Michael would heal better.

"I have a favor to ask."

"Of course, anything."

"Without any questions, we need you and Aden to come over to Michael's. By yourselves."

There was a pause before she responded. "I know you said no questions, but I have to know. Is it danger from Kayla or the other one?'

"No," Jordan answered. "It's nothing like that and no danger at all. It's something personal. Just come for coffee."

"Okay. Let me call Aden."

"Thank you, Olivia." Jordan ended the call.

She sighed and went to the kitchen to start a pot. Families and lives were so complicated. The Houses, which now included Michael, were some of the nicest and most decent folks she'd ever met. She hoped this wouldn't cause a rift between everyone. One never knew how even good people would react to such intimate information.

"Hey, God. It's me again." Jordan had grown up in the church. But when she got older, she'd drifted. Her own messy life and circumstances kept her focused on earth and not above. She realized in the past days since the accident how much she missed talking to God. "Please help Michael and his brother and sister find a way through this sticky situation."

"My mom used to pray like that. Just talk to him with no fancy words or gestures." Michael stood in the doorway of the kitchen.

"Feels good and right." She turned and leaned against the counter with arms crossed. "How's the head?"

He walked over and wrapped his arms around her. "It's all right. Hurts a bit. But you being here makes it better."

She rested her cheek against his chest. The dull rhythmic thudding was comforting. How close he'd come to that wonderful heart stopping forever.

About forty minutes later, the doorbell rang.

Barking exploded from the dogs in the yard.

"Good thing they were outside." Michael grimaced. "My head would have shattered at the noise."

"You, sit." Jordan pointed at him.

He was already pale and tired.

Geez, they hadn't even gotten to the most stressful part. "I'll get the door."

Ever cautious, she peeked through the glass before opening it. "Thanks for coming. Michael is in the living room."

"How's he doing?" Aden wiped his feet on the welcome mat and limped past her. "I know from experience how tough it is recovering from a bad accident."

"Me, too." Olivia followed. "Line us up, and we'll be like that Yankee Doodle 1776 picture."

"Let me take your coats." Jordan opened the hall closet and grabbed a hanger. "He's tired. In more pain than he'll admit."

"He should be resting." Aden helped his sister out of her coat and handed it to Jordan. "Not entertaining."

Jordan nodded. "And I think he'll rest easier after you talk."

"This is all very cryptic." Olivia frowned.

Jordan led the way to the living room. "Have a seat. I'll get the coffee and be right back."

While the usual questions began about how Michael was, she slipped away, then returned with a tray of piping-hot mugs, cream, and sugar. She sat on the recliner's arm, resting a hand on his shoulder.

When everyone settled in with their beverage, Michael began. "You know I've grown close to you over the past year."

Aden and Olivia quickly glanced at each other and then focused back on him.

"Are you breaking up with us?" Aden winked, but

the attempt at humor fell flat.

"I hope not." Michael reached up and rubbed the back of his neck. "But after I have my say, you may want to break up with me."

Olivia leaned forward, a vee forming between her brows. "Never. Michael, you're like a brother to us. Why would you say that?"

Aden stood and began to pace.

"I'm glad you feel that way, Liv." Michael took a deep breath and let it out. "Because I *am* your brother."

Aden froze.

Jordan handed the picture to the female House sibling.

Olivia took it, gasped, and then went over to show Aden.

"During girls' night at the condo," Jordan began. "I saw the picture of your mom and dad. At the hospital, I was given Michael's wallet. I opened it and saw that picture."

For the longest time, the only sound in the room was the ticking of the grandfather clock and the crackle of the fire.

Jordan rubbed Michael's shoulder. "Come back and sit down, guys. Can Michael tell you about it?"

The twins glanced at each other, and then Olivia took Aden's hand and led him back to the sofa. "We'd like to hear it."

"You know your parents went through a separation, right?" Michael's voice was soft.

"We do." Aden jerked a curt nod.

"Our mother told us they'd gone through a rough patch and spent a few months estranged." Olivia picked up her coffee cup with shaky hands but set it down without taking a sip. "Dad never talked about it."

Aden leaned his head back against the couch. "He probably felt guilty. And he should have. Did he leave your mother high and dry?"

"Don't be angry." Michael's features softened. "My mom never told him. She didn't want to come between him and his wife."

After he explained the same way he'd told Jordan about his parents, he finished with, "And I've been alone until this beautiful woman came into my life."

"I felt from the beginning that we had some kind of connection." Olivia got up and kneeled in front of Michael's chair. "And you'll never be alone again. Aden?"

The other man began pacing again.

Michael patted Olivia's hand and motioned for her to rise. He then stood and steadied himself. "Aden."

Jordan held her breath and prayed.

Aden paused and took measure of him. He nodded and approached, with his limp more pronounced. He grasped Michael's arms before pulling him into a hug. "Brother. I almost lost you without knowing. How messed up is that?"

Olivia sobbed a breath and hurried over to them.

The three siblings embraced, and tears streamed down Jordan's cheeks.

Family was everything, and she missed hers so much.

Chapter 22

Olivia slammed the office door as she exited. She went over to the bar and grabbed a tumbler, filling it with seltzer.

Jordan walked across the room just as her boss was stabbing a lime and sat next to her. "Hitting the hard stuff so early?" she teased.

Her friend grabbed both sides of the poor lime and wrung it into the glass. "Did I ever tell you I abhor Atticus Jones?"

"I believe you have. But this seems like more than your usual loathing." Jordan went behind the bar and tossed the desiccated lime into the trash. She grabbed a cloth and started wiping the juice away. "I'll play the friendly neighborhood bartender, and you tell me what's going on."

"I don't know whether to be scared, angry, or to laugh." She pulled out her phone. Swiping vigorously at the screen for a moment, she then turned it toward Jordan. "Look!"

Jordan took the phone. The food critic was posing in a picture with a leggy brunette in front of a restaurant. "Who's she?"

"That, my friend, is Kayla Lane." Olivia slammed the glass down, and liquid sloshed over the top. "And it appears she's surfaced close to home."

After handing back the phone, Jordan sopped up

the spill. "What's the big event?"

"It's the opening of a new restaurant." Her friend glowered while shredding a napkin. "Get this. It's called The *Premier* Jazz House." She made air quotes.

Jordan rolled her eyes. "Seriously? That is so lame. I think you should laugh."

The other woman's complexion turned a bit green. "I might if it wasn't for Kayla standing there."

Jordan dropped the cloth and hurried around the bar. "I'm sorry." She laid a hand on the other woman's shoulder. "That was insensitive. I'd feel the same way if it was you know who."

"We're a pair, aren't we?" Olivia covered her hand. "But we are women, and as you might sing..."

"We will survive," Jordan finished the lyric and pulled her friend into a hug. "And we will."

"Okay, enough sniveling about something we can't change." Olivia stepped back. "How's my—I can't believe I'm saying this—my brother doing?"

Jordan stepped up on the stage and adjusted the mic stand. "You know your family has hard heads? The doctor is amazed at his recovery."

"Well, Aden maybe." She touched the side of her head. "I don't know about mine. I don't know whether the pain is real or phantom. Sometimes I dream of being someone's hero. Not always the damsel in distress."

Letting out a puff of air, Jordan asked, "We have a lot in common, you and I." *Should I show her?* With only a second's hesitation, she lifted the side of her hair. "I get it. It's my question too."

Olivia gasped and joined her on the platform. "What is that from?"

"I'm not sure." She dropped the curl and lifted her shoulder. "Projectile, maybe. Could have been a bullet." With a flip of the switch, she turned on the digital piano and took a seat behind it.

"You could've died." A rogue tear trickled down Olivia's cheek. "I might never have known you."

"We each have our life's battle scars. You have your headaches." Jordan swiped the tear with her thumb. "Me, an actual scar. Aden has his limp. Michael will have his too. I think each person who goes on with their life after a bad incident is a hero in some way."

"A hero is maybe someone like Michael, who puts his life on the line." Olivia sat next to her on the piano bench. "Or David, who saves lives."

"One of the greatest vocalists ever has a song that reminds anyone facing difficulties that a hero is often as close as the reflection in the mirror." Jordan's fingers danced over the keys. After a few seconds, she said, "You are a hero. Mine."

"Tch, please."

"Hey." Without stopping, she glanced over at Olivia's bent head. "I had nowhere to go. No friends. I was scared to death."

"I gave you a job."

Jordan stopped playing. "Olivia, you gave me back a life. My music. You offered me not only friendship but unconditional love. You are my hero."

With a shrug, the other woman whispered, "Thank you."

Returning to the black-and-white keys, she started playing another song. It was a different rendition than the original. Still, she'd been working on it as a tribute to these people who rallied around her even at a cost to themselves. She sang softly. "What would you think?"

Olivia snorted. "I wouldn't stand up and walk out."

"Shut up, woman." Jordan nudged her. "I did a jazzy arrangement of this song with you, your brothers, and Shay in mind."

****

"Thanks again, Aden." Michael climbed out of the white sports car in front of the police department.

"You sure you won't need a ride home?" Aden pulled down his sunglasses and peered over them at Michael. "Your noggin okay?"

He smiled at his newly found and worrywart sibling. "I'm fine. The sarge said she'd give me a lift home."

His brother pushed the glasses back up. "Fine, but just remember I'm driving a cool car. What's she taking you home in? A minivan?"

He snorted and pointed to the lot across the street. "See the low red one?"

Aden whistled. "Is that a—?"

"Yep."

"Can she drive me home too?"

Michael gave him a casual two-finger salute and shut the door. He pressed the button at the front of the red-brick station house and looked up at the camera. Whoever was on duty buzzed him in, where he was met with clapping hands and cheers.

Heat flooded his face. "Come on, guys."

Vasquez was the first in line and gave him a huge man-hug. After him, a long line of shaking hands and well-wishes joined comments about how it was a good thing cops had hard heads.

"Swwwttttt!"

Everyone spun to face the sarge who stood in the doorway to her office swinging her brass whistle by the chain. "Machau, what are you doing interfering with the smooth running of my operation?"

She stalked across the worn tile floor while people scurried out of the way. Coming to a stop in front of him with hands on hips, she said, "You scared us." And then gave him a big ole family hug.

"Hey, Sarge." Michael's chest expanded, and he wrapped his arms around her. "Be careful. They may all think you have a heart under that uniform."

"Jerk." She smacked his back.

"Careful, I was wounded in the line of duty," he teased.

"Phft." Letting go of the hug, she didn't release him but held him at arm's length, looking him up and down. "You okay?"

"Yeah."

"Let's go to my office." She turned and led the way, only stopping long enough to shout, "Don't you people have work to do?"

When the door closed, Alyssa scanned him. "You're pale. Sit."

"I still get headaches. It's not unusual for someone to have headaches, dizziness, and problems with concentration and memory for weeks, even months later." He gratefully complied. "Olivia's husband, David, recommended an MRI just to be sure things were heading in the right direction."

"And?" She sat on the edge of the desk with her arms crossed.

"I'm good." Michael leaned back in the chair. "Better than most with injuries like mine.

Unfortunately, I won't be back to active duty for a while."

"Okay, but you're sure you don't just want to go home?"

He waved her offer off. "What news do you have?"

Alyssa nodded and circled the desk to sit. She picked up a pencil and twirled it like a baton between her fingers. "I spoke with some friends who have agents in strategic places. We know the feds already have DEA officers in the area, but what we didn't know was the surge in illegal narcotics activity is due to Vasilakis. Some Russian spilled his guts right before he died. Circumstances yet to be determined."

Michael leaned forward and rested his forearms on his knees. "Why haven't they taken him down yet?"

"The man is quite influential in not only business but political circles." The sergeant tilted her head and rubbed her forehead. "It is believed the Greek knows about Jordan. But no one knows when he will strike."

"So, what's next?"

"We wait."

Michael cursed.

Chapter 23

Jordan sat at the bar, sipping seltzer with lime while listening to The CorSam Trio laying down some sound in the loop station.

Since Andre appeared invested in them, they'd changed the name.

She breathed in scents coming from the kitchen. When she'd walked through a little while ago, Shay was preparing the ingredients. Jordan had spied the makings of a Creole gumbo lined up on the counter in their respective bowls. Now she could smell the onion, pepper, and garlic. If Shay nailed the okra, it was going to be good eating at Jazz House today.

Her phone vibrated in the back pocket of her jeans. She pulled it out and frowned at the unfamiliar number on her phone's screen, then swiped it open. "Hello?"

"Is this Jordan Vasilakis?" a woman whispered.

The world went fuzzy around her, and she grabbed the edge of the bar for support. "Who is this?"

"You don't know me, but I have a message from your husband."

Jordan's shoulders bowed forward, forcing down the sob that threatened to escape. "What do you want?"

"He wants you to go to Michael's house," said the woman. "Alone. And do not, I repeat, do not tell anyone. If you do, the cop gets hurt."

The line went silent.

.Jordan stared at the phone. Her breath hitched erratically. *No, no, no, no.*

She scrambled around in her purse for the keys to the new car she'd only gotten the day before. They fell from her fingers when she pulled them out, and she nearly dropped them again when she picked them up.

Glancing around to make sure no one was paying any attention to her, she walked to the hallway leading to the dressing room. Once out of sight, she bolted to the door. Inside, she shut the door and grabbed a composition book she always kept to write down song ideas. A pencil was tucked inside.

She couldn't leave without telling her friends and Michael. In shaky handwriting, she wrote a quick note, tore the sheet from the book, folded it, and stuck it in the side of the mirror. Olivia wouldn't be in for another hour at least. By then, Jordan would be dead or on her way back to Greece.

Hurrying through Jazz House, she waved and called to one of the early setup people, "I have a few errands to run. I'll be back later."

Once outside, Jordan ran to the old blue hatchback and climbed in. It took two tries to get the key in the ignition before the engine roared to life. Afraid of being pulled over, she forced herself to obey the speed limit until she got out of town.

The twenty minutes it took to drive to Michael's were torture. Several times she started to hyperventilate but forced her breathing to calm. She couldn't pass out.

When she reached the house, she pulled into the driveway and turned off the car. Silence. The dogs didn't bark.

Jordan gripped the steering wheel until her fingers

ached. If Kyrios hurt Michael or his beloved Forest and Jenny, there would be retribution.

She got out of the car. With her feet planted wide, her hands fisted, Jordan stared at the house. Her growing rage burned away any fear. No longer was she a pitiful, abused woman. Not only had she recovered the woman she'd once been, but now she was stronger.

"I'm here," she shouted. "Let's get this over with."

The front door opened, and the slim, dark-haired woman from the picture Olivia had shown her stepped out. "Are you going to stand there all day?"

"Who are you?" Jordan glared at her. "Where's Kyrios? And more importantly, where's Michael?"

"I'm Kayla." She answered. "It's freezing out here. Get inside."

"Where is Kyrios?" Jordan stayed put. "Where are Michael and the dogs?"

"Kyrios isn't here yet, and he doesn't know I am." Kayla crossed her arms. "And if you want to keep Michael safe, you'll come in and listen to me." She turned and went into the house.

Something about the woman's appearance told Jordan she was telling the truth. Dark circles under her eyes and the defeated posture reflected what she'd begun to think of as the Kyrios effect.

Jordan glanced from side to side. No sign of Michael's truck. The horses grazed, and there was no sign of Sherry, the barn help. She took a deep breath and steeled her will, then followed the other woman. Inside, nothing appeared out of place. "Where is everyone?"

"I got the dogs out of the fence earlier. The guy I'm working with took them. They're out of the way."

Kayla walked over to the window and peered out. "Michael got a phone call that they were in the Union County dog pound. He's gone to pick them up. It will give us time."

"Time for what?" Jordan pressed her palms to her eyes to stop the tears of relief. At least Michael and the dogs were safe. "Why are you doing this?"

"Kyrios killed someone I cared about." The other woman turned with a pained look on her face. "We only wanted a little money to get ourselves set up in a new place. It's what we deserve. But Kyrios found out about the plan and killed Oliver."

"Who's Oliver?"

"Oliver Brandt was my boyfriend."

Something besides tears gleamed in Kayla's eyes. Jordan remembered all the stories she heard in the past few months about this woman. Was she mentally ill?

"What do you have in mind?"

Kayla pulled a gun from her pocket. "I'm going to kill Kyrios. You're my bait."

Jordan backed up toward the door.

"No!" The distraught woman waved the pistol in Jordan's direction. "You're not going anywhere. Can't you see? This way will be better for you too."

"Kayla, take it easy." Jordan raised her palms toward her in a sign of peace. She needed time to think of a way out. "Of course I'll help you. What do you have in mind?"

"Good. I'd hate to have to hurt you. But I would." A phone appeared in her hand. "I'm going to call Kyrios in a few minutes. He thinks I'm on my way but won't get here for a while yet. I needed to talk to you first."

Thank heavens, the woman monologued as Olivia had mentioned. *Please, God, get me out of this.*

"Really, you have no role to play but to draw him in and keep his attention focused on you."

"Kayla, we should just get out of here." Jordan scanned the area for a weapon. The fireplace. "Look, over there on the mantel is a picture of Michael and me. We're a couple. He'll help us." She eased her way over to the stand holding the tongs, poker, and shovel.

"You don't know how he makes me feel." The other woman's voice cracked. "Like I'm nothing. But I'm going to show him. I want to see the look in his eyes and have him understand what it feels like to be helpless."

When Jordan was almost to the fireplace, Kayla waved the gun in her direction. "Stop moving. I'm going to call him now."

Jordan froze next to one of the chairs bracketing the fireplace.

"Yes, I got here a few minutes ago. She's here too." Kayla kept her focus on Jordan as she listened. "No. There's no one else around. We got rid of the cop like you instructed." Another pause. Then she pressed the phone to her chest and whispered. "He wants to talk to you. Don't let on. I don't want to have to shoot you before he gets here."

Jordan took the phone while eyeing the pistol pointed at her. She put it to her ear but didn't say anything.

"I can hear your breathing." Kyrios's Greek accent came through.

The sound of his voice made her blood run cold, but she refused to be cowed. "You couldn't just leave me alone."

"You belong to me," he shouted.

"I belong to no one."

"We'll soon see." Kyrios hissed. "Put Kayla back on."

She could barely swallow as she handed the phone back over. Kyrios was deadly when he was calm and quiet. She'd pushed him too far. His shouting made the acid in her stomach roil. She was in for a bad time. A very bad time.

"It's me," Kayla said. "Okay. Don't worry. We'll be waiting." She hung up and motioned toward the chair. "Sit. He'll be about an hour."

"What about Michael?" This had to be over before he returned with the dogs.

"From here to Lewisburg is almost two hours, plus bailing the dogs out? He won't be back until late afternoon, tops." The woman waved off her concern and started pacing. "When your husband gets here, you need to create a distraction. He'll have Tito, Anatole, and Luka with him. I'll have to take them out first."

Jordan sat, her hands twisting as she watched the crazed woman pace the floor, mumbling to herself. If Kayla had been teetering on insanity before, she'd fallen over the edge. "Kayla, they won't let you. His bodyguards are loyal. You'll die."

A car door slammed, and Jordan jumped at the sound.

Across the room, Kayla's head snapped to the front of the house.

Waiting for Kyrios to arrive was its own form of torment.

"That can't be him." Kayla looked at her watch.

"It's not been enough time."

Moments later, someone knocked on the door.

"Kyrios wouldn't knock." Jordan stood. "Let me see who it is."

"Don't try anything." Kayla poked her in the side with the pistol.

Jordan stumbled when the other woman shoved her. "Easy, I'm going."

Kayla stood behind the door while Jordan cracked it open. "Hailey? What are you doing here?"

"Hi, Madeline. I hope you don't mind me stopping by. I need a bit of help with a musical composition." Hailey looked over Jordan's shoulder into the room. "Can I come in for a minute?"

The gun poked her in the side. She flinched. "It's not really a good time."

"Madeline, are you okay?" The woman fixed her gaze on Jordan. "Can I help with something?"

"No, I have a headache is all." Jordan started closing the door. "Another time, maybe."

After shutting it, she peeked out. Hailey walked back to her car but stopped and looked around before getting in and pulling away.

"Kyrios should be here soon." Kayla jerked her head toward the living room. "Go sit on the couch."

****

Michael dialed the number to the shelter. He didn't know how the dogs got there, but when they texted a picture to him, there they were, behind bars.

This morning he'd found the gate open, and Forest and Jenny gone.

Someone must have taken them, then decided they were too much trouble.

Lucky for him the dogs were microchipped, and he'd kept up the registration. It was also fortunate that the animal control officer was an old friend, Heather.

She'd offered to meet Michael halfway.

He turned into the travel center near Drums to wait. His head was pounding, and if Jordan or Olivia found out he was driving so far—well, it was nice to have people in his life who cared.

Trucks and cars pulled in and out in a constant flow of travelers.

Finally, the green van with *Animal Control* in white letters pulled in.

Michael got out of the car with two leashes and waved.

"Hey, Machau," she called. "You lose something?"

He grinned. "Two troublemakers.

A ruckus began when Forest and Jenny heard his voice.

Heather climbed out and walked to the rear of the van. "Well, I'm glad we found them. Some loser tied them to the fence outside the shelter."

"Did you get them on camera?"

"Yeah, but not a face or vehicle, so it won't help locate him." She opened the back doors. "Looked like a single male. Seemed a bit prissy when he got dirt on his hands."

A rush of relief ran through his chest at the sight of the two furry faces. "You guys okay?"

Forest woofed, and Jenny wagged her tail harder.

"You sure know how to worry a guy."

Heather opened Forest's cage first, and Michael snapped on the leash.

Then it was Jenny's turn.

"I'd love to stay and chat, but when I told my supervisor about your situation, he gave permission to bring them but told me to come right back." She ruffled both dogs on the head.

"Yeah, I've got to get going too," Michael tried to keep the leashes from tangling. "Thanks again for all your help, and if you get any information on who had them, I'd appreciate you passing it on."

"Will do." She got back in the van. "Don't be a stranger. Give me a call, and we'll get together. Have a safe trip home."

He loaded up the dogs and got back in the truck. "Okay, you two, let's stop by Jazz House and see if Jordan is there."

Forty-five minutes later, he was in Jazz House's parking lot.

Olivia pulled in at the same time. "Hey." She walked over and gave him a kiss on the cheek. "What are you doing here?"

"Someone took my dogs this morning." Michael touched his cheek. Having a sister was one of the best things to happen to him. "I had to drive and meet animal control to get them back."

"What do you mean, someone took the dogs?" She peered in the window. "Are they okay?"

"They're fine." He frowned. "Not sure whether someone took them from the yard, or they got out and were found. Obviously, they didn't want them because someone tied them to a fence outside the Lewisburg shelter."

"Could it have been Kayla?" Olivia touched the side of her head. "She's back in town."

"Nah, she wouldn't know about our connection."

He turned her around, threw an arm over her shoulders, and led her in through the back door. "Come on, let's continue this discussion inside."

The CorSam Trio were practicing.

"Hey, guys." Olivia waved. "Sounds great. Have you seen Madeline?"

"She was here earlier," Coral replied. "Sophie said Madeline ran out the door looking stressed. We haven't seen her, and she's not answering her phone."

SammyD set his drumsticks aside. "She left a note stuck to the mirror addressed to you."

Michael sprinted to the dressing room with Olivia on his heels.

In the corner of the mirror, as SammyD said, was a piece of paper with Olivia's name on it.

He grabbed it and handed it to his sister. "What does it say?"

She took it, unfolded the note, scanned it, and gasped.

"What?" Michael took it from her shaking hand.

Dearest Olivia,
Thank you for all you've done for me. Kyrios has found me. Please tell Michael I love him. I have to leave before he hurts any of you.
All my love,
Jordan

"Where!" Michael dropped the note and ran his hands through his hair. "Where would she go?"

"I may be able to help with that."

Chapter 24

They both spun around.

"Hailey?" Michael blinked at the woman standing in the doorway. "What do you mean? How can you help?"

She reached into her back pocket and pulled out a phone. She swiped the screen and then said, "Lieutenant Morgan, I'm here with Officer Machau and Olivia House."

"Machau, listen up," came the familiar voice over the speakerphone. "Hailey is a federal agent. She's been working with us for a while."

The agent nodded. "We have someone else inside close to Vasilakis."

"Michael, I need you to take a step back from this," Morgan said.

"But..."

"No, you're too close and still injured," the lieutenant barked. "That's an order."

"But..."

"We'll meet you at the gas station on the corner two miles from your house. I'll give you a radio so you can listen in."

Michael tried to interrupt again, but Morgan wouldn't have it. "Not negotiable."

A short while later, Michael paced in the lot behind the gas station. "We need to get Jordan out of there."

Romano gave him the look. "Do not make me sit on you."

"But…"

"Michael, stop with the buts. You know once the feds are here, local P.D. is ancillary."

That's exactly how he felt. Secondary, maybe even third string. No use at all. According to Lt. Morgan, the Critical Incident Response Group, or CIRG, was now top dog.

Since finding the note, Michael's world had turned upside down. The woman he loved was in danger, and him? Helpless.

"Listen up." One of the CIRG men in black waved the others in. "We have our hostage team ready. Tactical is in place. The mark is about ten minutes out."

Michael rubbed his aching head. Ten minutes before either they got their lives back—or his world ended.

"Machau." Morgan approached. "I know this is hard. But they know their job. The house is surrounded by Feds, and Hailey is going to try to get inside."

Romano placed her hand on his shoulder and gave it a squeeze. "We would get involved if we thought they weren't up to the task."

Michael nodded. His head told him they were right. But his heart? His heart needed to get to Jordan.

"Five minutes." The tall guy in charge, one of three who wore a black suit with shiny shoes, notified them. "Agent Carter will be going in. There are two civilians inside at this time. The bird has eyes on the Greek. Two cars with three in the lead and two in the rear. Vasilakis is in the second vehicle."

"Who's Carter?" Michael asked.

"Hailey's real name." Romano turned from him and walked over to the local cops standing by. "Her real name is Molly Carter."

The rest of the blue-jacketed FBI agents checked weapons and headed for their vehicles.

Michael saw his chance. He grabbed his vest and off-duty weapon from the open door of the truck. If he was quick, his property was only a quarter of a mile as the crow flew.

He slipped around the gas station and took off through the woods. *I'm coming for you, sweetheart.*

****

The bonging of the grandfather clock in the corner was like a death knell. Each time it hit the quarter-hour, Jordan flinched and could hear her heart pounding in her ears.

Kayla continued to pace and ramble on about how unfair life was. How she deserved so much more. "And after Aden disappointed me, Oliver came into my life. He'd promised me so much. But I could have gotten so much more of what I deserved, with Kyrios's money. But no, he had to have Oliver killed."

The woman kept running her hand through her hair, and it looked like someone had dragged her through the bushes backward.

Kayla was unwinding in front of Jordan's eyes. At this point, she didn't know who was more dangerous. Kyrios or Kayla. She rubbed her temple. The woman's continuing mad ramblings made her head pound.

Movement outside the back door caught her eye. Hailey? What was wrong with that girl? She was going to get them both shot by the raving lunatic standing in front of the mirror, mumbling to herself. And Kyrios would be here any minute.

Steps sounded on the porch boards.

The door swung open, and Atticus Finch flew in, landing on his knees. He skittered over to the other side of the fireplace.

A tall man with shoulder-length black hair and icy-blue eyes followed him.

But Jordan focused on the devil behind him.

"Oh, my dearest Jordan," Kyrios drew the words out with a sneer. "How I've been looking forward to our reunion."

Jordan took the measure of the man who'd haunted her waking and sleeping hours. He'd grown jowly. Gray frosted his hair now, and the lines on his face gave him the appearance of an old wormy apple. Did he wear makeup for the cameras?

But she was done. He was a bully and nothing more. Because of his money, he'd been able to buy loyalty. She'd bet even Tito hated him. Besides, what more could he do? If she was going to die, she'd go out fighting. Not a doormat any longer.

Jordan stood with fisted hands. She was through with being afraid. "It's a reunion I could have done without. You've grown a bit paunchy there, husband."

His face grew so red she could imagine the cartoons where steam shot out of the character's ears.

"And you've grown a harpy's tongue. Oh, and you're not my wife."

She tilted her head to the side. "What do you mean?"

"I had the marriage annulled the moment I discovered you'd lived and disappeared. You've led me on a chase, and I'm going to make you pay."

"Why won't you just let me go?"

"But the game has been so much fun." Kyrios preened. "I come to the United States and make more money than you could imagine with their drug-hungry citizens. With the help of the business community and politicians, I could be a king here. And for dessert, I get to play cat and mouse with you. Good game. Now we go home."

Jordan shook her head. "I will not go with you. Kill me if you must, but I will never be your wife again."

"Oh, I don't want a wife." He chuckled. "I'm a happy bachelor, ask Kayla."

Chapter 25

Michael came through the tree line and peeked around the corner of the barn in time to see Hailey crawl through the dog door in the kitchen. It would have been funny if the situation weren't dire. He scanned the trees. There, in the maple. A camouflaged figure held a rifle with a scope.

The man saw him at the same time.

Michael pulled out his badge and flashed it.

He shook his head and signaled Michael to leave.

"Don't shoot me," he mouthed at the guy.

"Squad leader." The sniper keyed his shoulder mic. "We have a rogue cop up here."

Michael shrugged and took off for the house, making sure he came at it from the corner and out of the line of sight. He'd promised Jordan he would protect her. If nothing else, he was a man of his word.

When he reached the porch, he avoided the creaky board and crab-walked, staying low. He peeked through the window behind his leather chair, and his heart nearly stopped when he spotted Jordan facing down Kyrios.

Sweetheart, don't provoke him.

Out of the corner of his eye, there was movement.

Kayla stood in the corner. Her shaky hands pointed a gun at the Greek.

Before she could take the shot, Hailey appeared at

the kitchen doorway. "FBI. Put the weapons down."

"No!" Kayla spun and fired off a round. "He's going to pay."

Michael burst through the back door. "Police! Nobody move."

Jordan gasped as the woman sank to the floor with blood pooling around her. "Hailey, no."

Kayla waved the pistol around wildly.

"Put the gun down, lady," Michael ordered.

"No," Kayla screamed. She pointed it at Kyrios. "He has to be killed."

"Luka, what are you waiting for?" Kyrios snarled. "Kill her, and the man too."

When Kayla swung the gun at Luca, the man shot her.

Jordan clasped her hands over her mouth as Kayla, too, slumped to the floor, her eyes closed, lying still.

Michael counted the shots.

"Why did you hesitate?" Kyrios straightened his tie and glared at Luka. "She could have shot me. Now, kill him."

"We need an ambulance. An agent is down," Luka spoke into his collar. "And did you get all that?"

"Who are you talking to?" Kyrios narrowed his eyes at him. "You will answer to Tito."

"No, I won't. FBI. Put your hands up." The man pulled his wallet out and flipped it open. "You're under arrest."

Instead of complying, Kyrios yanked his own weapon out.

But as he raised it, Jordan grabbed the shovel from the fireplace. And like she was Jackie Robinson, swung it full force, striking the back of her ex-husband's head.

Kyrios hit the floor and sprawled at her feet.

The front door burst in, and the room filled with people wearing blue jackets emblazoned with FBI. "FBI! Down! Down! Everybody on the floor."

Michael laid his weapon on the floor and held up his hands. "I'm police."

"Yeah, I know you, and the only reason I'm not cuffing you is that bulldog of a sergeant." One of the suits glared at him. "But I don't envy you. She can't wait to chew you up."

The police cuffed the unconscious Kyrios.

Jordan was on the floor next to Hailey. "Come on, open your eyes."

"Is it over?" The woman opened her pain-filled eyes. Is anyone else hurt?"

Jordan looked up at Michael.

He nodded.

"Yeah, It's over." Jordan brushed the hair away from the other woman's face. "And you should only worry about yourself."

"Sweetheart, are you okay?" Michael glanced toward the door. "Because I think they're taking me outside to have a word."

"Yes." Her voice trembled. "I'm staying with Hailey for now. Are you all right?"

"Yeah, I'm good."

"Machau." Lt. Morgan, trailed by Romano, stalked toward him. "Outside. Now."

He followed them out.

A while later, unsure how much time had passed, Michael leaned up against one of the vans used to carry the FBI agents. His head pounded, and his hands shook.

Red-and-blue lights lit up the front yard.

Even though he was law enforcement, they'd escorted him out of the house. After they took his statement, the suits left him alone. But the stress and activity took their toll now that the adrenaline had worn off.

He scanned the area looking for Jordan. There she was, standing next to the stretcher, still holding Hailey's hand.

Thankfully, the agent was stable.

Kayla, though, had been airlifted to the hospital.

The paramedics said she was in critical condition.

"Jordan!" He paced over, ignoring the pounding in his head. When he reached her, he grabbed her in an embrace, burying his face in her neck.

"Michael," she murmured, throwing her arms around him before pushing away and running her hands over him. "You look terrible. Come, sit."

He was grateful to be led to her car next to the ambulance. She popped open the hatch with the key fob, and he sat.

"Are you crazy?" Worried eyes scanned him. "You should let the medics check you."

When she went to wave one over, he grabbed her arm. "No, I'll be okay."

"Are the dogs okay?" She took his face in her hands.

"You're cold." He covered her frigid fingers with his. "They're fine." Holding her at arm's length, he scowled. "What about you, you crazy woman?" He scanned her. "Are you hurt?"

"No, I'm fine." She reached over to the woman on the stretcher. "Thanks to you, Hailey"—she glanced around and then pointed to a man standing and talking to Lt. Morgan—"and Luka."

"Who's Luka?"

"Undercover."

"Molly, thank you. Zack, how bad is she hurt?" Michael looked at the EMT tending her arm.

"She'll be fine. The bullet glanced off the body armor and nicked her shoulder. That's where all the blood came from."

"Hurts like a sucker, though."

"Molly? Who's Molly?" Jordan asked.

"Me." The woman being swathed in a bandage by Zack answered. "It's my real name. Right, Zack?"

"You two know each other?" Jordan tucked herself under Michael's arm.

Zack blushed redder than a clown's rubber nose. "Yeah, we go way back."

Shouting from the house distracted them from the two googly-eyeing each other.

"How dare you." A conscious and cuffed Kyrios appeared on the porch surrounded by federal agents. "Do you know who I am?"

No one responded to his continued cursing and threats, and Kyrios was placed into a black SUV.

Funnily enough, it was similar to the one Michael noticed driving around town. Just not as fancy.

Hours flew by before they were allowed back into the house and then, only the kitchen.

Olivia and Aden had arrived a little while ago.

"Michael, come stay at my condo or Aden's." Olivia fluttered like a mother hen.

He tried to hide a smile. "No, the investigators are nearly done, and the clean-up crew is on its way. Besides, I have the dogs and need to take care of the horses."

Someone knocked at the kitchen door, where his family congregated.

"Can I come in?" Alyssa Romano stood in the doorway.

"Come on in, Sarge." Michael waved her into the room. "Everything is winding down, and we're discussing what happens next. We're having coffee and some cranberry pecan coffee cake, courtesy of Margaret, that Aden brought with him from Rock House."

Alyssa shoved her way through. "Margaret's? Stand away from the cake, and no one gets hurt."

Everyone laughed but nodded in understanding. Mags was the best pastry chef in the world.

Jordan started another pot of coffee then stood behind him, resting her hands on his shoulder. "How's Kayla?"

"She'll live." Alyssa shook her head. "That girl is messed up. After she recovers, she'll go back to jail. Atticus Jones filed charges against her. His now-deceased cousin, Oliver, and Kayla blackmailed him. They were going to implicate him in all the incidents from last year's debacle with the assaults on the Houses and their businesses. Then Kyrios got to him. Atticus is planning on a long vacation."

Michael leaned forward, resting his arms on the table. "Do you know what happened with Anatole and Tito?"

The sergeant heaved a sigh. "Anatole is in custody. Once the shots sounded from the house, the FBI descended like locusts. Swooped in and took him. We have evidence he's the one that hit you with the SUV."

"And Tito?" Jordan pressed. "He's never far from Kyrios."

"Tito was never in the car. No one knows where he is."

The coffee pot pinged that it was done, and Jordan stepped away from Michael to pour more. Her voice shook when she asked, "What about Kyrios?"

"Luka has been working with the International Operations Division of the FBI for a while." Alyssa took the mug from Jordan. "He's been able to get a great deal of information. Enough that the charges should stick to Kyrios this time. Plus, we have him on record from today's incident. You may not be forced to testify. I don't know if the law will stand, but marriage has its privileges. However, the spousal privilege is not absolute and comes with several exceptions and conditions."

"It's okay." Jordan put the coffee pot down. "We're not married. He had it annulled last year."

Jordan reached out to Michael.

He rose and gathered her in his arms, holding her while she sobbed. "It's over, sweetheart. Finally, you're getting your life back." He prayed that her life would include him. She was so talented the world would be at her fingers.

Chapter 26

Everyone had gone home, leaving her alone with Michael. She was exhausted, but there was no way she could sleep until she called her mom and grandma. She had to tell them before the news broke.

"I need to call my family, but it's going to be so hard." Jordan sat in the rocker across from Michael on the front porch late that night. Both needed to breathe the clear air.

The chemicals from the crime-scene restoration company still lingered.

"You do." Michael took a sip of the herbal tea she'd made. "But only when you're ready."

Flames lit the porch from the fire burning in the chiminea, which threw off enough warmth to keep them comfortable.

The dogs sprawled at their feet. It was past their bedtime.

"They're already done mourning me."

Michael shook his head. "No, they aren't. You're their family. Their blood. You never get over mourning family. Trust me. I think of my mother every day. I see her in people's kindness to others. Sometimes in their smile. It gets easier with time, but it never stops completely."

The moon was coming up over the trees, and she remembered. "Grandma quoted this to me once, *Your sun shall no more go down, nor your moon withdraw itself; for the Lord will be your everlasting light, and your days of mourning shall be ended."*

"I love your grandma's quotes." He leaned forward. "Let their yearlong mourning be ended."

She nodded and pulled out her phone. They were an hour behind, so it wasn't quite as late in Louisiana. She waited while the phone rang.

"Hello?" Her mother's soft southern accent was hesitant. No good call would come in at this time of night. When Jordan hesitated, the voice became a bit sharper. "Who is this?"

"Hello, Mama." Her voice cracked. "It's me, Jordan."

Silence.

"Mom, it's me."

"If this is some kind of a joke, I'm not impressed."

"No, really." Jordan panicked. "Mama, don't hang up. It really is me."

"Jordan!"

She jerked the phone away from her ear when her mother screeched.

Shouting on the other side ensued, "Oh my Lord. How can this be? Mom, Mom, my baby is on the phone."

Shouting and crying continued on the other end.

Jordan got up and began pacing the boards, waiting for them to calm down. It took everything she had to stay calm.

"You're pacing. The House family seems contagious," Michael teased her.

She attempted a smile.

"Are you there?" Her mom's voice shook. "Jordan,

where are you?"

"I told you she couldn't be dead. I'm her grandma. I would know."

She could hear Gram in the background. "Mom, please." Poor Mom was trying to reel Grandma in.

"Jordan, where are you? What happened?"

"I'm in Pennsylvania." Tears started flooding down her cheeks. "I want to tell you all about it. But not over the phone. In person."

"Are you well? Who are you with?"

"I'm with friends." She swiped her face with a sleeve and looked at Michael. "And one special friend I want you to meet."

He beamed at her while nodding.

"Is it that Kyrios?" Mom tsked and huffed. "I knew he wasn't good for you."

"No, Mom. Don't worry about him. You might see some stuff on the news. Just remember I'm safe." She crossed back over and stood in front of Michael. "I'm with Michael. He's a good man. You'll like him."

Moi? He mouthed.

Jordan ruffled his hair and covered the phone. "Yes, you."

He kissed his finger and touched her lips. Then pulled her into his lap, rocking while she reconnected with her family.

They talked for a bit longer about her work and living in Pennsylvania. The other stuff could wait for a face-to-face. Right now, her mom and grandma both needed assurances that she was all right. And she needed to hear their voices after so long. But now Jordan was even more exhausted, though this time, it was for a good reason.

"Look, Mom, it's been a long day and late here. We have some things to tie up in Pennsylvania, and then we'll catch a flight down."

"Call me tomorrow." Her mom sounded like she was sniffling again. "I need to know this wasn't just a dream. Ouch! Why'd you pinch me?"

In the background, Jordan's grandma said, "So you know it's not a dream."

"I'll talk to you tomorrow." Jordan laughed and hung up. Curling up in Michael's lap, she nestled her head against his chest. "I'm kinda like Ma. I'm worried this is a dream."

"Do you want me to pinch you too?"

"How about kissing me instead."

"You have the best ideas." He lowered his head, paused to peer into her eyes, and said, "I love you."

Chapter 27

The next few weeks blurred past. After Michael and Jordan gave their statements to the police and depositions to the lawyers, there wasn't much else to do, so it was the opportune time to go visit her family.

Michael was cleared by the doctors to fly, and Sherry said she would house- and dog-sit.

They stayed a week, the three women laughing, crying, and catching up.

Michael was embraced like a son. He would miss them when they returned.

Grandma even gave him a Matthew Henry quote. *To a good man, God gives not only wisdom and knowledge but joy.* Then she thanked him for bringing joy not only to Jordan but to her and Jordan's mother.

When it was time to leave, tears flowed once more.

Michael didn't know there were so many types of tears and how long it could go on.

Jordan's mom and her grandmother made them promise to come back soon.

Now, out on the trail behind his property, reality hit home. Usually, riding the trails gave him peace. Still, even though the woods were ablaze with forsythia, snowdrops, blue violets, and buttercups, nothing chased away his nerves.

He touched his pocket again. Hoofbeats kept time with chirping birds as he barely noticed the Flowering

Dogwoods and Redbud blossoms through the still nearly bare branches of the maples and oaks. This could go either way.

"It's so pretty up here." Jordan tilted her head back, and the sun shone down over her, making her look like an angel. She inhaled deeply then turned to smile at him. "Smells good too."

"Yep."

Eyebrows drew together as she pulled Rose to a stop and spun the mare to face him. "What's wrong with you today? Aren't you happy it's all over?"

"Olivia said another talent scout showed up at the club." Michael kept going and reined Jack around one of the white Flowering Dogwoods. He could feel her eyes on his back.

Jordan sighed loudly and clucked at the mare, catching up to him. "Yes, they did. So what?"

"And?"

"Honestly? I wish they would leave me alone." She almost whispered the words.

"I thought it was your dream?" Michael frowned.

"Look, there's our rock." She pointed to the boulder where she'd shared with him about Kyrios. "Can we talk?"

Michael's shoulders slumped. "Okay.

After he'd lifted her onto the stone surface, he turned and leaned against it with his arms crossed over his chest. "This is where we say goodbye, right?"

"What? No." Her voice was incredulous. "Michael, I thought you were acting distant. Why would you think that?"

He walked away, digging both hands deep into his pockets. "Because it's your dream to be on stage.

You're free now. There's nothing to hold you back."
He steeled his will. There was no way he'd keep her
from her hopes and dreams. "And because no
relationship has ever worked out for me."

"Michael."

Two slim arms wrapped around his waist. Her
cheek pressed up against his back.

"Haven't I made it clear how much I care about
you?"

"Yeah, but things have changed." He turned and
looked down into her eyes. "I refuse to stand between
you and your dreams."

She lifted her hand and laid it alongside his cheek.
"Dreams change. I'm not the girl I was."

"But you still have dreams, don't you?" He pressed
into her palm.

"Yes, but different ones." She gathered his hands.
"Ones I'd hoped you had as well."

"What are they?"

"Let's walk and talk. I don't like that rock
anymore."

"Okay." He gathered up Rose's and Jack's reins.
"C'mon, guys."

****

Michael's words cut like a knife. She slid off the
stupid hard rock and approached him from behind. The
dreams of a young woman living in the spotlight had
faded. Jazz House was where she wanted to be
professionally. Friendship with Olivia, Shay, and the
CorSam Trio filled her with satisfaction. Being with
Michael? Like that green Christmas villain, her heart
grew three sizes every time she was with him.

After a few moments of silent walking, she bent

and picked a yellow coltsfoot. It wasn't a daisy, but it would do. *He loves me.* Pluck. *He loves me not.* Pluck.

"I used to dream of being famous." Jordan admired a wispy cloud shaped like a feather. "Being on stage. Making albums and hanging out with others in the business."

"I heard used to," Michael's voice was soft. "No more?"

"My grandmother, the one with all the quotes…" She rubbed her hand over her heart, missing her. "She always says, 'Be careful what you wish for. Because you just might get it.' "

"Mom used to say the same thing." Michael glanced over at her. "They were right. There things I wished for that now I'm glad I didn't get. It's like that country song. The one thanking God for not answering his prayers."

"I know the one you mean." Jordan hummed then sang a few bars. Her voice cracked when she said, "Sometimes, I wish he hadn't answered mine. But then, I never would have met you."

He pulled her to a halt. "What are your dreams now?"

"I love working at Jazz House." She stared at the ground. "Olivia and Shay are like the sisters I never had."

"What else?" His voice was gruff.

"A cabin in the woods." The backs of her eyes burned from holding the tears. She let them go.

"Being surrounded by family." Jordan stopped walking and turned. She reached up and cupped his cheek. Looking into his eyes, all she saw was love. She threw herself into his arms. "A good man who makes me laugh. Who loves me as much as I love him."

"I'm that man." His arms wrapped around her. "I'll always be that man if you'll let me."

"Michael."

Their lips crashed together, and she could taste the cherry candy he always carried. She slid her hands up his biceps, over his shoulders and neck, and tangled her fingers in his dark hair. Jordan's heart pounded. And it wasn't because they'd been horseback riding that her legs turned to linguine under her.

He teased her lips with his mouth. Nipping at her, then taking her bottom one and tugging gently but firmly with his teeth.

She opened to him. How long had they stood there exploring? She had no idea.

His arms loosened, and Michael took her face in hands that covered her from chin to hairline.

Soft brown eyes looked into hers, then butterfly kisses covered her eyes, nose, and cheeks.

They stood staring at each other until Rose headbutted her in the back.

"Horses only have so much patience with humans." Michael steadied her then rubbed the back of his neck. "Since you're not breaking up with me, I'd like to ask you something."

"What?"

There in front of God and the horses, he got down on one knee. "Jordan Welles, I love you and want to spend the rest of my life with you."

"Oh, Michael."

He reached into his pocket and pulled out a box. When he opened it, the sun flashed off the stones. "Will you marry me?"

"Yes, Michael." She pulled him to his feet. "I would love to marry you."

Chapter 28

Michael peeked out from behind the screen in the little circa 1920s chapel. The seats were filled and the overflow area too. The pews, draped with garlands of green, were highlighted with red and white dahlias.

Out in the seats, he spied Alyssa and her husband, Matteo. Lt. Morgan sat next to them. Shelly had cleaned up after taking care of the horses and was with a gentleman he didn't recognize. Zack was there with Hailey…no, Molly?

Sweat trickled down his back, and he tugged at his collar.

"How you holding up, brother?" His best man, Aden, laid a hand on his shoulder.

Straightening, he stepped back. "I'm good."

"Really?" Aden snorted. "You look a little green."

Michael ran a hand over his head. "It's a full house. What if she changed her mind?"

Now hands rested on either shoulder of his black tux while Aden peered at him. "That woman loves you. She'll be here."

Michael looked at his watch. "It's five minutes past."

"Women have a lot to do to get ready. She'll be here."

The side door opened, and Alex Rodriguez, who also agreed to stand with Michael, slipped in. "Jordan and the other women just pulled up."

Taking a deep breath, Michael blew out air. "Thanks, man."

"Let's go over it one more time." Aden pulled a list out of his pocket. "I have the ring. Do you have your vows?"

He patted his pockets and started to panic. "I-I-I…

"Check your inside pocket, Machau." Alex opened Michael's tuxedo jacket and pulled the vows out. "Chill, man. It's going to be fine."

His heart began to pound, and he tugged at his ruby-colored bowtie as the first bars of the music started. Jordan hadn't wanted a traditional processional, so together they picked a beautiful song about how long they would love each other.

"It's time." Aden rebuttoned his coat and straightened his tie. "You good?"

Michael swallowed and nodded.

Alex went first, followed by Aden and then Michael. The pastor stood at the top of the three steps. They lined up as people hushed and turned to the rear of the sanctuary.

The door opened, and Shay walked down the aisle first.

Michael smiled at her, and she winked back at him.

"*My* girl." Aden poked him. "Yours will be out in a minute."

Michael elbowed his brother and whispered, "Shut it, Rodriguez," at the snickering man.

When Olivia came through the door, he rubbed his chest. *My sister.* She was gorgeous, and a thrill ran through him at the adoring look on David's face. She deserved that kind of love.

The vocalist joined the music, humming at first before asking, "How long will I love you?"

His throat tightened, and he whispered, "As long as the stars," before he choked up.

A vision in white. Her gown was somehow sleek and modern yet reflected her inner jazz woman.

****

Jordan touched the white 20s-style headband with ruby-red stones, making sure it was still in place. Olivia and Shay had fussed until the white dress was perfect. The sleeveless flapper style dress fit loose to the dropped waist and then to a mid-thigh hem. Its fringe reached the ground.

Shay's hazel eyes sparkled. "You're stunning."

"Isn't she?" Olivia handed Jordan the red-and-white bouquet of her favorite dahlias. "It's almost time."

The musical interlude started, and Shay slipped through the door first. Olivia was next. Both looked stunning in ruby-red high-low dresses.

Jordan took a deep breath. She loved the song they'd chosen, and when the vocalist began to hum, she did too.

The double doors opened wide, and the congregation stood.

Murmurs ran through the crowd.

She didn't have to paste on her stage smile. A real one stretched from cheek to cheek. These were her friends and family. Her heart did that thing again and grew three sizes.

Eli and Margaret represented Rock House Grill. Next to them were the staff from Jazz House.

She nodded and gave a little wave. Farther down,

she could see all the people from Michael's department.

Alyssa Romano actually threw her a kiss.

The CorSam Trio were near the front. Coral in her signature color from head to toe. Did SammyD polish his head? Andre was understated as usual.

Mother and Grandma were showstoppers in the colorful Afro-Brazilian dresses her mother had made from material she'd saved from Jordan's dad. It was like a piece of him was here too.

Then her gaze fell upon her heart—Michael. The look in his eyes nearly undid her. She took a stutter step. Love blazed, and she reached for him.

He took her hand and whispered, "You are the most beautiful woman I've ever seen."

"You're looking pretty dashing yourself."

Michael kissed her.

A throat cleared. "We didn't get to that part yet."

"Sorry."

"Sorry."

"No problem." The minister nodded at them while indicating where they were to stand.

Olivia stepped forward and took the bouquet.

"Ladies and gentlemen, please be seated," Reverend Bill instructed.

Whispers faded, followed by rustling as the congregants settled into their seats.

"First, I'd like to begin by welcoming everyone and thanking you for being here on this happiest of days. It's no accident you are here. Each is invited because you represent someone important in the individual and collective lives of Jordan and Michael.

"Under God, we are a human family. Sometimes we forget that. But each of you has been created to love and support your families, friends, and neighbors across this place we call earth. Here, today, we meet as this couple joins together to accomplish this. As the Word says, *Two are better than one, because they have a good reward for their labor. For if they fall, one will lift up his companion.*

"The couple wishes to read their vows together. Is that still correct?"

"Yes, Reverend, we do." Michael stepped a bit closer to Jordan.

Olivia came forward and handed her a piece of stationery while, with a shaky hand, Michael pulled his notes from a pocket.

Knowing he wasn't fond of public speaking, Jordan leaned in and whispered, "Easy, big guy. You're going to be great."

They unfolded the papers and faced each other. She gave a slight nod, and they began.

"I, Jordan…" she opened.

"And I, Michael…" he continued.

They gazed into each other's eyes. Neither needed the papers.

"Take you to be my partner in life and my one true love. I will cherish our friendship and love today, tomorrow, and forever. I will trust you and honor you. I will laugh with you and cry with you."

Jordan's voice cracked, but Michael's nod of encouragement helped her push through.

"Through sickness and in health. Through the difficult and the worse, for richer and poorer. Whatever may come our way, I will always be there for you. I have given you my hand to hold. I give you my life to hold. I place my heart in your care from this day forward."

Weeping could be heard from the audience.

But they weren't done.

Michael cupped her cheek and then turned to face those in the pews. "We have something we'd like to do."

Jordan walked to her mother and grandma. She reached out. "Can you both come with me?"

Surprise lit both faces, but without question, they took Jordan's hands, and she led them to the front and up onto the platform where three candles stood. Only two flickered. The one in the middle remained dark.

Then it was Michael's turn. "Aden and Olivia? Will you both join me?"

The brother and sister looked at each other. This didn't happen at the rehearsal dinner the night before.

Reverend Bill joined them at the table. "As I said, we are all together in this. Jordan and Michael would like you all to light the Unity candle with them.

Momma, Gram, and Olivia now had tears running down their cheeks. Aden looked so stoic, but Jordan could see him trying not to cry.

Three hands grasped each candle and moved toward the dark one as the pastor spoke. "Love is patient, love is kind. It does not envy, it does not boast, it is not proud. It does not dishonor others, it is not self-seeking, it is not easily angered, it keeps no record of wrongs. Love does not delight in evil but rejoices with the truth. It always protects, always trusts, always hopes, always perseveres."

The middle candle now shone brighter than the others.

"I now pronounce you not only husband and wife

but one family." He leaned toward Michael and in a stage whisper said, "Now's the time. You may kiss your bride."

Cheers erupted.

"What, no quote, Ma?" Jordan's mother whispered.

"No, all that needed to be said was."

Madeline's Song

There's an ocean of space between us
And across this great divide
My heart aches to be secured
Love's yearning to come alive
If stars could control our destiny
I'm sure they'd let us be
Shining on our love
Blessing you and me
Past choices and decisions clash
With wishes of today
Now is not the time or place
So I must go away
If stars could control our destiny
I'm sure they'd let us be
Shining on our love
Blessing you and me
What we feel cannot survive
Not with who we are
Our paths on separate roads they lay
Traveling the opposite way
If stars could control our destiny
I'm sure they'd let us be
Shining on our love
Blessing you and me
You stand so close, I've only to reach out
But I snatch my hand away
Go out, my love, and find your joy
You must turn away
You must turn away
I must turn away

A word about the author...

D. V. Stone is a multi-genre author. In April 2020, The Wild Rose Press released *Rock House Grill*, followed by a July 8th, 2020 release of *Rainbow Sprinkles*, part of the One Scoop or Two series. She is also independently published with *Felice, Shield-Mates of Dar*, a fantasy romance. Soon, *Kisa*, the second book in the Shield-Mate series, will be available. *Agent Sam Carter and the Mystery at Branch Lake* and *The Mystery at High Pointe Tower* are middle-grade paranormal.

Around the Campfire is a popular weekly blog where she reviews books by other authors and shares her favorites in a monthly newsletter.

Recently retired from full-time employment in a medical office, she's wife to an amazing husband, mother to one son, and not your average grandma to three beautiful grands. A woman of faith, D. V. believes and trusts in God. When not behind the wheel of 2Hoots—a 41 foot long 13.2 feet high 5th Wheel camper—she rambles around town in Northern New Jersey in a white Camaro.

"My greatest pleasures are spending time outside with friends and family, cooking over the open fire, sipping a glass of wine, and reading."

Hali, her rescue dog, always reminds her to let readers know, "Woof, woof." Which is loosely translated as support your local animal rescue.

http://dvstoneauthor.com

Thank you for purchasing
this publication of The Wild Rose Press, Inc.

For questions or more information
contact us at
info@thewildrosepress.com.

The Wild Rose Press, Inc.
www.thewildrosepress.com

www.ingramcontent.com/pod-product-compliance
Lightning Source LLC
Chambersburg PA
CBHW060542260626
47161CB00003B/1013